# *the* Rainwoman

God's blessings,

*Jay R.*

Soli Deo Gloria

J.C. McKenney, MD, FACS

# *the* Rainwoman

Tate Publishing & *Enterprises*

Published by Tate Publishing & Enterprises, LLC
127 E. Trade Center Terrace | Mustang, Oklahoma 73064 USA
1.888.361.9473 | www.tatepublishing.com

Tate Publishing is committed to excellence in the publishing industry. The company reflects the philosophy established by the founders, based on Psalm 68:11,
*"The Lord gave the word and great was the company of those who published it."*

Book design copyright © 2010 by Tate Publishing, LLC. All rights reserved.
*Cover design by Amber Gulilat*
*Interior design by Stefanie Rooney*

Published in the United States of America

ISBN: 978-1-61663-134-5
Fiction, Christian, General
10.04.12

# DEDICATION

This book was written in the hope that it might give a glimpse of the greatness of God. Beyond that, it is dedicated to the missionaries of Hospital Loma de Luz, past, present, and future who have sacrificed so much to further God's work there. Chief among these for me will always be my wife, best friend, and partner, Rosanne, and our children, Nate, Gabe, and Hannah.

# FOREWORD

You might think it rare that someone like me should be introducing a book. I do not have any titles. I had to leave school after *Basico*. That would be like your ninth grade of school. I do not own a bank. I worked in a bank once. I mopped the floors and cleaned the bathrooms.

I'm not famous and I'm not an expert on anything. But I have lived enough to have some stories. And I do have a voice. And I know something about this book, because I know the hospital and I know the people in the story. They are people like me who have never been asked to introduce a book.

I know the people in this story because they are just like the people I grew up with. I was born and spent my childhood in a little village in the campo. The people in this story are like my neighbors, my grandmother, my aunties and uncles and cousins. I have a mountain of cousins. Many of them still live in that village. I do not think anyone ever asked any of them to make an introduction for a book: just me.

I know this hospital because I spent two months there with my daughter. And I thank God for it every day. *Primero Dios* (first it was God) I have to thank. After Him, it was the good people of that hospital who gave me back my daughter, Andrea Elisabet, mi *lucera del alba,* "my morning star." Since the first moment I saw her she has been the light in my day. Her friends call her Lisabet. To myself I call her *mi lucera.*

Andrea Elisabet is twelve years old now. She was ten when she was burned. On the 22nd of April two years ago I was at work. Andrea Elisabet was on her way home from school. She passed some boys on the street that were playing with a fire in a pile of branches and leaves. One of them kicked a can of paint thinner into the fire, and it caught my daughter as she passed by. I will never forget, for the rest of my life, seeing her for the first time at our neighbors', all wet from the lagoon she was smart enough to jump into. Her skin was hanging off of her little arms like wet paper. She told me not to worry, not to cry.

At the private hospital they wanted twenty thousand lempiras before they would even see her. I did not have twenty thousand lempiras. At Atlantida (the public health hospital) we spent the night in the hallway with everyone else. We still had not seen a doctor when my neighbor called. She had an aunt whose husband had lost his job. Her aunt had just the day before come to stay with my neighbor until things got better.

That morning they were talking about Andrea Elisabet. She told my neighbor that she had been cared for at Hospital Loma de Luz. She said that they would not turn Lisabet away. I have a cousin who drives a taxi. After two weeks working on it, he had just gotten that taxi running that morning. I took her straight out of Hospital Atlantida. He took us all the way to Loma de Luz. It cost three hundred lempiras, the last that I had. Lisabet was not conscious by then. She was breathing very fast, and her heart was racing. I'll tell you I have never been so desperately afraid. At the hospital gate the watchman called the nurse on duty. She talked to the doctor, and they let us right in. They didn't ask us for money. They just took her straight to the emergency room.

For the next two months they cared for mi lucera in that hospital. I lived in their sanctuary housing for a time. She went through five operations. It was a very hard time for us. But at the end, I went home with mi lucera. She is in school now and wants to be a nurse. Thanks be to God.

I tell you this much of my own story to introduce the story of the book. Andrea Elisabet and I heard the story of *The Rainwoman* in the hospital. In those long hours between dressing changes the nurse from the operating room read from the manuscript in English and translated the story into Spanish. Now I am telling her my story for the introduction to the book. I suppose this experience makes me an expert in something. I know the kinds of people in the book. I know the kinds of people in the hospital. And I have seen that God uses small things, like a man losing a job, or the hour when the taxi gets fixed, to make good things happen from them: like the raindrop.

These are real people. They have a voice. And this story keeps faith with them. I suppose in many ways they are not so different from you. Maybe we are not so different from the ones who are usually asked to introduce a book. Because I think that in all of our lives God does work from moment to moment in these tiny things that we cannot see, yet He moves mountains with them. This I have seen in my life and the life of my daughter. I pray God should bless you, as he has blessed us.

–Mari Elena Robles Mejia

# AUTHOR'S NOTE

This is a work of fiction. The characters and the events are all based upon actual people and occurrences. But neither the characters nor the events portrayed in this book are based completely upon one specific person or one actual event. I have endeavored to avoid portraying the specifically identifiable while remaining true to the characters and the story: the story of the severe and shining grace of God shown in a special place for a people that He surely keeps close to His heart.

# CHAPTER ONE

Why is light given to those in misery, and life to
the bitter of soul?

Job 3:20

Misery is a sickness of the soul, born of pain accepted,
grown in fear endured, fed from hope left too long
out in the weather. One can surely die of misery. Or
your life might just turn on a raindrop. Magdalena
very nearly died of misery. But she didn't. No, her life
turned on a raindrop.

Toward the ragged end of *la temporada de lluvias,* "the time of rains," the storms of winter had
so soaked the coast of Colón that there was no clear
distinction between the shifting gunmetal gray
above, the dark and silent water table beneath, and
the sodden, dripping landscape in between. From the
worn and broken Cordilleras to the south, across the
narrow coastal plain, to the wild and lonely beaches,
like Magdalena, everything was soaked through to

the bone. Magdalena had come back, back to the last place she ever wanted to be, back to the last place left for her to go. With nothing left to lose and nowhere else to go, she had come back to the place where her brief and brutal life had begun.

Las Niguas it was called. Even the name, a regional appellation for a particular trombiculid mite, a small biting and burrowing insect, even the name bespoke the worst of the *campo*. It was a place Magdalena had come to despise early on. An hour's bus ride from the nearest paved road at Jutiapa, then another half hour's foot travel up the path to Las Niguas at the dead end of a dirt trail going nowhere else but nowhere. It was here at the end of the last path to the rest of the world, on the doorstep of the mountains, that her mother *la dió a luz,* as they say. "She had given her to light," given her birth, and then left her on the doorstep … not that there was a doorstep, for the floor was dirt where Magdalena's mother had left her. The floor was dirt and the door was of *caña brava.* The floor was dirt, and there was no step up from the packed earth *solar* outside the door. Inside there were too many other mouths to be fed, too many other needs to be met for Magdalena to be noticed much or often by her tired *abuelita,* her worn-out mother's mother, the only adult in the house where she had been left.

Magdalena could still see that little girl sitting by the door, looking down that path, waiting for her mother to come back for her, hoping that she was special to someone. But she never did. Her mother never did come back. It made Magdalena angry how it still hurt. Some ten years before, that anger had been enough to push Magdalena down that path and away from the mountains behind. But anger wasn't enough to sustain her in the end. The anger, like most everything else, had been used up, paid out, or leaked away, leaving only the hurt. Now it was all just a part of the misery.

A lot had happened to Magdalena in ten years. The vague hopes she had left with left first. Anymore, she couldn't remember clearly the outlines of what her hopes had been. Like dreams after awakening, they had lost their hard edges, their specific characteristics, and had become mostly symbolic. Maybe her dreams had never been very clear. But she had somehow dreamed of a safe place, clean and light—a place with enough food—a place where it didn't seem like something terrible was always just about to happen.

By the time she had left her abuelita's house, she was almost thirteen years old. She had given up on her mother coming back for her. At least she told herself that she didn't ever want to see her. But, at almost thirteen, Magdalena still hoped for someone who thought she was special, someone who thought she mattered. At almost thirteen, a man more than twice her age gave her just enough reason to believe that he might be the person who cared for her ... who thought she mattered. Magdelena never knew his proper name. Everyone called him *Chele,* an Indio term for someone relatively fair skinned. There was a fair amount of English pirate blood on the north coast of Honduras. Sometimes, where it was least expected, it came out. Although course and pock-marked, this Indio's skin was paler than most. His good eye was a murky green. The other was milky white from an injury as a boy. Chele's voice was high and nasal, and he spoke and moved like a dog that had been kicked too much. He smelled like the onions he sold out of the back of someone else's pickup truck. But whenever he came around, he had something he said he had been saving for Magdalena. Usually it was a *bon bon,* a cheap sucker on a paper stick. But sometimes it was a magazine of the *Telenovelas,* "the soap operas," and once it was a compact with a mirror and a lipstick.

One hot and tiresome day, a week and a half after the gift of the compact and the lipstick, Magdalena sat beside the door with the lipstick on her lips and her things tied in a bundle at her feet. Every single person in that house (there were nine at the time), walked past her without noticing her … every single one. No one noticed the lipstick. No one noticed the pitiful bundle at her feet. When her *abuelita* shuffled past without a word or even a glance, Magdalena stood up, clutching her little bundle to her chest. She walked slowly and stiffly across the hardpacked dirt of the solar and then continued on down the path. Faster and faster she walked. Then she ran and ran and ran. Down the path, down along the river, down toward the main road at the crossing of the Rio Esteban; she ran like someone desperately needing to get somewhere. But she had nowhere to run to. She wasn't running to; she was running from.

Earlier in the morning, Magdalena had heard the battered Toyota pickup with no muffler that Chele drove, passing on the route out to *Rio Coco.* As she ran along the river's edge, she could hear it crossing the broad shallow river at the fording place. Now on its return trip, she could hear it struggling up the western bank. She could easily hear Chele's amplified, nasal singsong calling out the virtues of the vegetables under the tarp in the truck bed as he rolled slowly past the trail to Las Niguas and into the edge of La Colonia Margerita: "*Repollos, cebollas, papas, papas, papas, pataste, tomates, fresco, fresco, fresco!*" Chele was coming back from the end of the road at Rio Coco. He was heading back toward the west, selling what vegetables remained as he passed through the little villages strung along the coast road like the beads on some tawdry necklace, with knots and gaps in between. Magdalena knew as she ran that if she caught him in time, Chele would let her ride with him as he headed west, away from the house where nobody noticed, away from these mountains, west toward real cities and the rest of the world.

So she ran as her tears dried. She ran while her lungs burned. She ran though her gut ached. She ran until she caught Chele on the west side of the Colonia. She had no wind left to ask or explain. She just climbed in over the tailgate and rolled in with the potatoes, carrots, onions, and cabbage. Chele looked back through the cab window, smiled, and steadily accelerated. The transmission ground and clanked as he shifted up into third. Magdalena didn't look up. She looked at her feet, clutching her little bag, which held her other dress, her worn shoes, a comb, the compact with the mirror, and the lipstick. She kept her face set and never looked up to see the mountain above Las Niguas getting smaller and smaller. She never looked up until they had turned the bend; other mountains intervened, and she could see it no longer.

It took ten years for Magdalena to complete that journey. Ten long years had passed since she had left her abuelita's house, angry and hopeful, proud and scared. That young girl, pretty innocent and innocently pretty, that young girl was long gone. Ten years of hard work and hard weather had passed out in the campo. But in the city, a lifetime of abuse and exploitation, a lifetime of continuously lowered expectations, of tedious boredom and sudden violence, of drugs and prostitution or the bartering of one's soul, which amounts to the same, had so changed Magdalena that no one from Las Niguas would have ever recognized her … if anyone from Las Niguas had ever looked for her. For many years, that life had made her hard and tough, and a little crazy, her heart hidden away in some place that no one would ever find. Even Magdalena had forgotten where she'd hidden it. But when her health and strength had failed her, the hardness, like the anger, had just leaked away. It left her broken and used up, ruined and wasted away. All that was left was the misery.

Still, we don't die that easily.

Magdalena could not have said why or what she was hoping to see, but one rainy morning in San Pedro's Colonia Rivera Hernandez, she stared into the cracked mirror in the filthy bathroom down the dark tenement hall from the room where she stayed. She stared in, and what she saw staring back startled her out of her stupor. She reached out to touch the glass where it reflected the worn and battered woman's face that once had been kind of pretty. She whispered, "*Pobrecita*." Her hand suspended over the glass, she thought of her abuelita, who had sometimes said that when Magdalena was hurt as a little girl: *pobrecita*, "poor little one." At the moment her finger touched the cold glass, she sensed deep inside that she was dying. She looked down at the rusting razor on the side of the washbasin and thought, *Maybe I should just finish it here.* Then her hand fell from the mirror and came to rest on her belly. She left it there, in that posture that all women heavy with child have stood in, feet spread wide, left hand behind tired hips, right hand resting on that improbably distended belly. For the first time in months, the fog of drugs and alcohol and the drudgery of just staying alive lifted a bit. She felt the baby kick her right in the palm of her hand. It startled her a little and focused her attention deep inside.

Deep inside, she focused her attention on *the someone else* within her. For a long pause she didn't breathe, and it seemed that her heart waited to beat, and then the baby kicked again. That second kick, the one she was paying attention to and the one she held her breath for, started some reconnecting of broken pieces, the sum of which scared Magdalena. She hadn't been scared in a long while now. The baby's kick started a tear tentatively, silently wandering down her hollow cheek. She hadn't wept for a long time either.

The words that came into her mind were *No puedo aguantar a dejarle aquí.* "I just can't bear to leave the baby here." It was what she couldn't put into words that scared her. Without words, she realized that by choosing to live so that the baby could live, she was choosing to care. And if she cared, she risked her heart getting hurt again. No, if she cared, in this life, her heart *would* get hurt again. That is what scared her. But the baby stirring in her womb communicated some subvocal but undeniable will to live. Magdalena just could not ignore it.

So began Magdalena's long and perilous and exhausting journey back to the beginning of her journey, back to the foot of the mountains. Not that Magdalena longed for those mountains, it was just the only place she knew where her baby might have a chance. That chance, she knew, was less than small. But here in this moldering house in the worst part of Colonia Rivera Hernandez on the outskirts of San Pedro Sula, she knew that she would die. And then, the baby would die. And they would just haul them both to an unmarked grave at the *cemeterio nacionál.* She just couldn't let that happen. The baby wanted to live.

Magdalena sold her cooking pans, her chair, her sheets, her forks, and her knife. The old electric stove top belonged with the room, but she sold that too. Even so, she gathered so little that on the day she left, the first day it didn't rain all morning, she walked. She walked the three miles to the causeway because she didn't want to use the forty *lempiras,* the two dollars it would cost to catch the *rapidito* for the ride out.

Once at the causeway, she sat in the sun, on the side of the road at a *punto de bus* for an hour and a half. Once again, all of her belongings were stuffed into a pitiful little bag at her feet. Then the bus, *El Progresso,* pulled to the roadside and sat idling long enough for her to board. The bus was already packed with at least seventy other pilgrims and their assorted belongings. She was neither strong enough nor quick enough to get a seat. So Magdalena stood sweating and struggling for balance until she switched buses at the *maquila* ( the clothing assembly plant) El Porvenir just east of El Progresso. The second-class "express" bus to *La Ceiba* from there on was a little less packed. A plump and garrulous woman filling out a shapeless cotton dress pushed the hen she was carrying in a sack off the seat. She scolded and swatted her two oldest children with the shoes she was carrying, and they dutifully gave up the edge of the seat to Magdalena.

By the west side of *Tela,* everyone was seated. From Tela on, Magdalena had a seat to herself. Exhausted, she slept on her side until San Juan

Pueblo. There the bus was forced to stop for repairs.
The second of the double right rear tires blew on one
of the *tumulos,* one of the speed bumps in San Juan
Pueblo. After some discussion, they flap-flap-flapped
through town with all of the passengers pressed onto
the left side of the bus (to take the pressure off the
right rear rims). They pulled into the *Copena* station
with the wrecked busses out back. When Magdalena learned that they also had a restroom out back,
she was so relieved that she cried. Pregnancy does
strange things to anybody.

One of the two right rear tires was easily repaired.
It just needed a sizable patch on the already heav-
ily mortgaged inner tube holding up the worn-out,
"tubeless" tire. The second tire was beyond any rem-
edy that could be offered in San Juan Pueblo. So a
deal was struck to buy one of the tires off one of the
wrecked busses out back, and an hour later, they were
back on the road again. Magdalena lay back down
on the bus seat in the back, curled up around her
hopes and fears, curled up around an empty and nau-
seated stomach. She curled up around the new life
within her that so wanted to live. She curled up on
the second to the last seat over secondhand tires on
a second-class bus, and slept the dreamless sleep of
the dead.

She slept through the last of the mountains. She
slept past Pico Bonito, its *cumbre* shrouded in cloud.
She slept on through the pineapple fields and the
city traffic. At 4:43 p.m., the bus pulled into the *centro de buses* in La Ceiba, four hours and forty-two

minutes after it had pulled away from El Porvenir. Under the circumstances, the chauffeur was rather pleased with himself to have made the 162-kilometer run so efficiently. It was by no means his best time that month. But it also wasn't his worst.

Like the dead, Magdalena slept on while the living filed off the bus. She slept on until the chauffeur's *ayudante,* the driver's "helper," nudged her with his foot, saying, "Hey! Mami! You can't sleep here! Now go on, get off!" Without a word, Magdalena struggled to her feet. Flat-footed and sleepy-faced, she waddled down the aisle and sidestepped the long steps down to the pavement. She stood looking around the parking lot without a clue what to do next. She didn't think about luggage. She had none. All that she owned was either on her or in the orange and white striped plastic bag that she carried, rolled and tucked into the crook of her arm.

Not knowing where to go, but feeling vulnerable standing there, Magdalena began to walk. She walked by the big promenade of *tiendas* that served the bus travelers. Many poor *campesinos,* if they ever traveled into a big city like La Ceiba, never ventured out from the block of the centro de bus. Many of them thought that this actually was the city of La Ceiba in that one block. There, they could find a market for their wares or produce. There, they could splurge on food they usually didn't have at home: *baleadas,* or *carne asada* with flour tortillas, or roasted ears of corn with salt, or those little *calientitos.* In the market of the centro de buses, they could buy anything from cheap clothing to cheap hardware, to the cheap rice and salt they needed back out at the other end of the bus trip.

The centro de buses came to life about five a.m., but it began to prepare for bed about five p.m., and Magdalena arrived just too late. The shop keepers were fastening their wooden shutters. The families that slept in the back of each twelve-by-sixteen-foot tienda were preparing their own suppers. They stared briefly with stony faces at Magdalena as she walked past. Then the *dueña* would turn her back without a word. The teenage girl would throw the pan of dishwater just behind her feet. The little dogs would bark and snap, and the grandfather on the chair wouldn't say a word to stop them. They had served people like this all day long. They could tell that there couldn't be much money in that plastic bag, and so, no reason to stay open.

Magdalena walked on. She walked out and turned down the Avenida Quince de Septiembre. Ignoring the pair of stooping taxis that slowed and honked for potential fare, she turned toward the center of town. With years of training in passing as invisible, Magdalena looked directly at nothing but the ground in front of her feet. She listened to everything but responded only to the dangerous sounds. She thought about what she could eat that wouldn't make her sick, where she could sleep that might be safe, and what she could do to protect the life within that depended on her.

When Magdalena began shuffling down the

Quince de Septiembre, the sun was low in the sky behind her. She kept following her long, thin shadow until it became so thin that it faded from sight. The walk seemed interminable, and she began to have to take rests at bus stops and storefronts. When she reached L'Avenida de La Republica, the dark was overtaking the dusk. By the time she reached the *parque central,* the luna moths and the bats, like small comets, were weaving erratic orbits around the streetlights. Feeling that she could not take another step, Magdalena assumed *Domenio Util,* squatter's rights, over a bench in the back corner of the parque near the Cabildo, the city government building across from the big Iglesia San Isidro. It seemed like the best of her very limited options.

From her perch on her bench, she silently watched the old men playing dominoes on the benches along the Avenida San Isidro. They were later supplanted by young men drinking beer who made loud, crude comments about the women in the passing cars and laughed and cursed at the street evangelist pleading and sweating in his cheap suit. Later still, the lovers had left. The drugs and the money had changed hands, and the street children came out. In the small hours of the morning, one of them tried to grab her bag and run, but Magdalena bared her teeth and growled like a wild animal, and he ran away empty-handed. Her heart fluttered in her ears, and she began to cough. The tail end of the night passed in weary naps on the hard, cold concrete bench, punctuated by coughing spells. Finally, the breath of first light blew the dark from the battlements of the Cordillera Nombre de Dios in La Ceiba's southern sky. Too tired to move, too wired to sleep, Magdalena watched the dawn descend from the mountain tops. She felt utterly spent.

# CHAPTER TWO

When I lie down I say, "When shall I arise?" But the night continues, and I am continually tossing until dawn.

Job 7:4

Magdalena lay on her side with her face on the hard bench, eyes open, staring straight ahead. Gates were unlocked. Traffic started up. Gaggles of school children in navy blue pants and skirts and white shirts began to walk by or ride by on bicycles. Still, Magdalena stared straight ahead.

She was tired and weak and sick and afraid. The tired and weak and sick part held her to the bench. She did not believe she could get up. But she was also afraid. In the tug-of-war of motivations, *fear* often proves stronger than tired or weak or sick. She was afraid of staying. She knew she could not risk another night in the city without shelter. She had no food, no money she could afford to spend, no safe place, and no way to get any of these things here. Fear won out. So, arising with her sisters all over the world, a disheveled and dirty street woman struggled up off a park bench in the city of La Ceiba, Honduras. Like a wraith that belonged to the vanishing night, she arose and shuffled off, and, still staring straight ahead, she disappeared.

Keeping the mountains of the Cordillera Nombre de Dios to her right front, she turned east and south and worked her way toward the banks of the Rio Congrejal, the old eastern boundry of La Ceiba. Passing through the fruit market in La Colonia El Sauce, she found some rotting mangos in a trash pile. She ate the parts that seemed still good. At the edge of the entrance to the old bridge that the Indios called El Puente Saopin, all of the rotten mango came back up. In the morning light on the side of the road, she wretched until she thought she'd turned herself inside out … and all that was left was the taste of acid and rotten mangos. She wiped her mouth with the back of her hand and walked herself across the bridge, across the river, and out of town.

In a "developing" nation, like Honduras, the cities are not a condensation of the industry, culture, and commerce of the rest of the country, similar to the countryside but more concentrated. Instead, the cities are islands of modernity; such as it is, surrounded by the sea of the rural world. Rural Honduras continues on at its own pace, the culture at an earlier stage of development. Magdalena was now headed out into the countryside, the *campiño,* or *campo* for short. Up to this point in her journey, many of the people in Magdalena's story have been self-centered, ungracious, closed, and hard. It is true, Honduras has its share of such people, particularly in the stagnant and polluted waters she has so desperately been struggling through: *los aprovechadores*, the takers, the violent, the indolent, the *mareros*, the *vagabundos*, the *malcreados*, the people who had taken their advantage of and used Magdalena these past ten years, the ones who then discarded her. But, on the main, the Honduran people are not like this. They are, generally speaking, a gracious and generous people; hospitable, and given to identify with and care for the disenfranchised, the humble, the *humilde*. This is particularly true where Magdalena was now headed, out into that sea of rural Honduras, out into the *campo*.

The journey from the city of La Ceiba to "*el medio de quien sabe donde,*" (the middle of nowhere), like Las Niguas, can be compared in many ways with traveling back down a timeline. Its passage goes through stages connected by the string of time and distance. Each stage is predicated by a set of expectations. The expectations in many ways are based upon the common mode of travel. Close to the city, there is the stage of housing developments. It assumes a certain degree of affluence that allows for private automobiles. Each house has its own private driveway, its own electric meter, its own telephone service, its own patch of yard, its own walls and gate. Further out lies the stage of hotels and resorts. Here, taxis and rental cars are assumed. Distances to tourist attractions and to the airport are known and posted, but one assumption is that guests will stay at the hotel, eat at the hotel restaurant, and swim at the hotel's beach and pool until time to go on a guided tour or return to the airport. The local buses only stop at the one entrance to each of these stages ... to let off and pick up the domestic workers, the yard boys, the bell-hops and cooks, who, of course, live elsewhere in real places with their own different assumptions. Further still, the highway begins to pass through places and ways of life that did not develop as a result of the highway, but pre-date it. There the highway is not an integral part of the place, it has become merely a thin line connecting the dots of real communi-ties that exist independently. The highway connects these communities by bus and truck to distant cities, but once you step off the pavement, transportation is all local (usually by foot or bicycle). The assump-tions, interests, and relationships are all local, inter-related, and of long standing.

Magdalena eventually left the highway at just such a village: a village called Jutiapa. Jutiapa is the Aztec name for the place of the Juti people. As you can tell by the Aztecs naming it, the pueblo predates the highway. She had reached Jutiapa in the back of a once-green Toyota pickup that appeared to have pre-dated the Juti people. The pickup was owned and operated by a farmer from El Portillo. The farmer, who was taciturn by nature, had a tooth that was really bothering him so that now you'd be lucky to get four words per hour from him. So, when he spotted

Magdalena walking slowly and unsteadily down the roadside at Las Hamacas, just outside of La Ceiba, he thought (but didn't say) *Pobrecita*. Coming to his decision, he had slipped the clutch and coasted the creaking and rattling old truck past Magdalena to a dowdy but dignified moorage in the dirt parking lot of El Restaurante Las Hamacas.

The once-green Toyota suffered from a malady common to older vehicles venturing down the highways and byways of Honduras: the Oblique Directional Disorder, or O.D.D. Due to a torque in the frame from some previous or cumulative series of mishaps, accentuated by the use, out of economic necessity, of a random assortment of tire sizes on the same vehicle, trucks and buses suffering from O.D.D. point in one direction but actually move forward on a course several degrees off of their apparent heading. The end result is a somewhat unsettling diagonal drift down the highway.

Having pulled off the road on such a diagonal drift, the old farmer waited idling there in the morning sun until Magdalena caught up. Realizing he was offering her a ride, she climbed in over the remains of the tailgate. There she sought out a place among the dogs, the spare truck parts, the empty milk *tambos*, and the farmer's extended family. Once sure she was settled, though still without saying a word, the old man carefully looked up and down the empty highway, then let slip the mooring lines, tacked obliquely out of the parking lot, and slowly careened back across the westbound lane. They gradually picked up speed and set on all sail for points east.

In the middle of the truck bed, up against the cab, was a battered metal desk chair with armrests still intact but the legs cut off. It was secured to the wooden truckbed with screws and brackets made of angle iron. Its seat was padded with feed sacks. Enthroned on this permanent addition to the truck was a stocky, gray-haired woman, the sister of the old farmer, the *abuela de la paila*, or grandmother of the truck bed. In this part of the world, the bed of a pickup truck is a *paila*. *Abuela* as you probably already knew, is a grandmother. This abuela de la paila, the farmer's sister, liked to keep a close eye on her grandchildren, grandnieces, and grandnephews. They naturally rode back in the paila, so that is where, from her throne just behind the cab, the abuela ruled the roost. Besides, she preferred it out where it was cooler and certainly breezier. "Mas fresco alli" (it's fresher out there) she liked to say. At any rate the front, the *cabina*, was occupied by her sister-in-law (the farmer's wife), who didn't like the window opened. By the time they had reached Jutiapa, the abuela de la paila had thoroughly questioned Magdalena in her friendly but regal way regarding where she'd grown up, who she knew there, where she had been, and where she was going. By the time they had reached Jutiapa, the abuela de la paila was thoroughly worried. This very pregnant young woman, all skin and bones and baby, obviously sick, had no money. She had no food, and the abuela wasn't sure that the young woman knew anyone who would care for her if she ever got to where she was going.

The old Toyota land schooner pulled into the *Punto de Buses,* the bus idling area on the side of the highway, at the edge of Jutiapa, down in the Valley of the Rio Papaloteca. The vendors hawked their wares to passing travelers: seasonal fruit (sometimes peeled and salted mango slices, sometimes *nancis* and *manzanitas* in little plastic bags), wrapped plate lunches, bags of chips, drinks in bottles or plastic bags, and the occasional iguana. The abuela de la paila bought a plate lunch for the exorbitant price of twenty-five lempiras, carefully counting out the exact change from a roll of small bills from a battered leather pocketbook she kept deep in her skirt pocket. She also gave one lempira, fifty *centavos* to each grandchild to buy a bag of *churros* or a *toporillo.* She insisted on praying with/for/over Magdalena there in the paila before she got out. Then, once Magdalena's feet were securely planted on the pavement, she gave her the plate lunch she had bought. Magdalena, embarrassed, almost smiled and mumbled her thanks, but she was too sick and too exhausted for her thanks to be as gracious as the gift.

Next, in the traditional manner, Magdalena sidled up to the driver's side window to ask how much she owed him for the ride. She knew she had no money to spare and hoped that the farmer would say that it was *por nada,* for nothing, (in the traditional manner). The old man took her thin, young hand in one of his big gnarled ones. He patted her hand with the other (the one missing a finger and a half) and so between the two hands he passed to her a folded ten lempira note. Magdalena was again too groggy and too unaccustomed to kindness to know how to respond, so she stood there staring blankly at the old man. The farmer seemed to understand, smiled anyway, wished God's blessings on the little waif, then found first gear, and obliquely headed back into the eastbound lane of the road to Trujillo. The abuela de la paila and all of her grandchildren, grandneices and nephews waved to Magdalena through the trailing little cloud of blue-black exhaust smoke. They watched her standing there at the Punto de Buses, holding her plate lunch and the ten lempiras in her palm, getting smaller as the truck struggled up the hill heading obliquely on toward *Trujillo*.

Magdalena turned her thin back to the highway and faced down the main street of Jutiapa. It was only three blocks down that street from the highway to the old railroad bridge over the Rio Papaloteca, and the entrance to the dirt road out to Colón. Still, it took Magdalena nearly an hour to get there. She stumbled along in the haze and ache of a high fever. She stopped every twenty or thirty paces to cough and catch her breath … each time starting again only because she couldn't think of what else to do.

She climbed the cutoff road past the Funerales Garcia and on up the old railroad embankment to reach the row of shabby *pulperias* (open-front general store kiosks) perched there on the bridge apron. She sat there panting on a plank bench under the eaves of the last pulperia in the row. Yet even after twenty minutes on the bench, she could not regain what it had cost her just to climb the embankment. Her thoughts, like a too-tired swimmer, would surface, sink, and then struggle to the surface again in desperation. *That's blood,* she thought of the metallic taste that strengthened each time she coughed. *For how long now?* she wondered hazily. A little while later, she thought, *It's starting to rain.* After some time passed like this, her mind cleared a little, her thoughts treading water near the surface. She learned from listening to the fluid crowd at the roadside that: (a) she had missed the three o'clock bus, (b) there was one more bus of the day, (c) that would be the five o'clock bus to Rio Esteban, and (d) it costs twelve lempiras.

Magdalena had the ten lempiras the old farmer had pressed into her hand. She had 490 lempiras secreted away in her clothes. That was all the money she had in the world, four hundred and ninety lempiras, which at the time was equal to about twenty-three dollars. That was all she had *entre ella misma y el tigre* as they say, "between herself and the tiger of hunger." She was determined to save that money for as long as she could. There were pickup trucks that passed by at irregular intervals. Over the next hour, two stopped and accepted passengers. Magdalena considered it but hesitated, not knowing if she could get up, not knowing if she could stand the rough ride in the paila of a pickup in the rain. She hesitated too long twice and missed those two opportunities.

Then came a long wait with no traffic passing … just the rain dripping from the eaves of the little store's corrugated tin roof in a steady drizzle. It was going to be dark soon.

When the five o'clock bus came splashing up through the *charcos,* the mud puddles, the conductor leaning on his horn, Magdalena decided she had to chance it. She would offer the ten lempiras she had in her hand, hoping they wouldn't throw her off for the two lempiras she couldn't produce. She couldn't spend the night there on the bench. The bus paused on the bridge's western access long enough for Magdalena to climb the three high steps from the ground, and then pulled onto the bridge as she took a seat halfway back on the half-empty bus. She stared out the window, fogged on the inside, mud-drenched on the outside, the wet campo passing by beyond. The ayudante didn't come by to check destinations and collect fares until they were slowing for the tumulos at Diamante de Zion. When he turned to Magdalena, she answered, "Las Niguas" and held out the ten lempira bill. "*Es todo lo que tengo.*" "It's all that I have," she sort of lied. He looked in her face for a moment with eyebrows raised and lower lip out, then took the ten and moved on down the aisle without a word.

"Las Limeras, Las Crucitas, Lis-Lis, Bejucales, Balfate, San Luis … " and the muddy way continued, a run-on sentence punctuated only with rain-soaked, miserable little commas, rolling stops on their way further and further out into the campo. The gray daylight darkened gray-blue through gray-violet, and the indigo mountains crowded the road right down to the sea.

The last minutes of the day found the bus hesitating on the western bank of the Rio Esteban. One of those unexpected but welcome windows had opened in the curdling and shifting storm clouds overhead, allowing the sun to paint the sodden world golden red for a moment. Leaving his shoes on the seat behind the conductor, the ayudante jumped off the bus and walked sideways down the muddy bank to the river. With his eyes on the currents, he carefully waded out to midstream then turned and retraced his steps. The water had soaked his pants up to just above midthigh. Both the driver and the ayudante knew well that above waist level was too much of a risk for sucking water into the air intake of the bus. By the feel under his feet, the ayudante could distinguish between loose sand and well-packed sand on the bottom of the Rio Esteban. By the feel on his legs he could judge the current. Judging depth, current, and bottom of the bridgeless wild rivers of this isolated circuit was a routine part of the ayudante's job. He didn't need to explain much. As he climbed back up the steps, he nodded to the driver and declared the rain-swollen river to be passable. The door shut. The headlights were lit. The bus slid down the bank, plunged into the river, and plowed on across the ford like a matron pushing through a waist-high field of grain. She downshifted, climbed up the far bank, shook herself, then headed on into the dusk toward the end of the line … leaving Magdalena alone on the western shore. She stood there watching the bus out of sight, then turned her back to the road and began her way up the path, up the river that she had last run down ten years earlier.

Before the last light left this abandoned end of the world, the track heading up the river toward the *aldeas* of the mountains was easy enough to discern. But it was murder to navigate. It was by no means a way for vehicles, and never had been. It was a *caminito,* a "little road," essentially, a common-property public footpath. In the summer, it might be rugged and ungraded, but it would, for the most part, be hardpacked clay with roots and rocks and brush chopped out, or pulled out, or detoured around. The sides of the caminito with the weeds and branches would be kept cut back by the passing expert swing of a thousand trips of men, women, and children bearing sharp machetes. But in the rainy season, it was a slippery, overgrown, rutted obstacle course. The cattle and horses and burros which were driven or ridden or ambled down this path in the summer, also did so in the winter. But in the winter their hooves sunk deep in the mud and cut deep into the banks which the rains washed down into the path in a lumpy porridge. The passing beasts also contributed some of their own lumps. And in the winter, travelers hurried on to get out of the rain while the brush grew thick and dripping at the edges.

Magdalena slowly picked her way around and over and through the obstacles. It was a *legue,* just over three miles, up the caminito from the coast road to the path leading to the doorstep that Magdalena had run away from ten years before. It had taken her less than twenty minutes to run down to the western bank of the Rio Esteban that hot summer morning. It took her nearly two hours to crawl and climb back up it. Even then, she had missed the turnoff path on the first pass. The occasional on-again, off-again drizzles had turned into a constant mist. The last of the twilight was gone. The dark world closed in, and the track became even more difficult to navigate. Magdalena picked her way along the lighter darkness of the track between the greater darkness of the vegetation on both sides toward the utter darkness of the mountains. The disorienting noise of a chorus of a million toads and frogs on all sides was incredibly loud ... parting only slightly for her passage, closing in behind her a minute later. The occasional sudden crash or rustle of something in the brush near at hand would have startled her time and again, if she had had anything left for that. She finally found the side path to her abuela's house, largely by groping with her hands. There was a gap in the *madreado* trees there. A barbed-wire gate, a *falso* that bridged the gap was laid to one side, and an old cow path meandered between, but the whole way was overgrown and choked with months of growth. It took Magdalena another fifteen minutes to make certain that this was the path and to be almost certain too that this was no longer a path that people used.

The one hundred footsteps between the caminito and the solar, between the public path and the front yard of her childhood home, though paced out with fewer good memories than hard ones, were not forgotten. This was the place written on the DNA of her childhood memories. As Magdalena retraced the path she knew by heart, even overgrown and in the dark, she relived it. She had thought that she had lived past the pain of looking back. But when she reached the head of the path, despite what her mind already knew, as she stepped out into the open area that had been the yard, the desolation took her breath away. She thought that the pain and the fear would stop her heart. As she slowly turned a backward circle, she whispered to the emptiness, "¿Ni aun este? ¿Ni aun este?" "Not even this? Not even this?"

Deserted again, she knew she had gambled her last centavo and lost. She had risked all that was left of her to get to this place, forsaken by God and man and beast, on the chance that someone might take her in … and there was no one there. She had gambled and lost and knew she was too sick, too broken, too spent to get back to where she'd been even two days before.

The little house was a collapsed ruin, overgrown in *sarce* and *bejucos*, "thorn bushes and vines." The little *champa* beside it, which they had used for milking the cow, still had a roof. But the *manaca*, "the thatch of the roof," was rotten, and the rafters destroyed by termites and half of them bending or fallen inward. The roof of the champa shed the rain so poorly that the floor was almost as wet as the mud beyond the dripline. Leaning back against one of the posts that held up the remains of the thatched roof, Magdalena slid down to sit on the floor of damp dirt and old cow manure. She stared off into the darkness in misery ... a misery deep enough to die from.

She stared up into the black heavens, where the rain kept coming from for a long while. She thought of what she knew of death: of cold, washed-out bodies in cheap clothes in cheap caskets surrounded by weeping women, of dogs and *zopilotes*, "buzzards," fighting over swollen carcasses. She thought of hell and wondered how it would be worse. The burning must hurt. She thought of God and knew she knew even less about that. She thought he must be high up and far away beyond the rain. She looked up to where that might be and had no hope that he might hear. But she rasped out a barely audible "please?" A gust of wind blew the rain back in her face, and she blinked. In less than the time it took to blink, in less than the time it took her tired eyes to close and then automatically open, that faraway God heard her whispered one-word prayer. That faraway God who had been sitting with her for hours, heard her prayer, determined a way, and chose to take the risk of changing the course of a raindrop for Magdalena. But it would take a little time. There was a lot to do.

A few hours before dawn, Magdalena could no longer feel her legs or hands. In a sick stupor, she had been sitting there for hours, feet out before her, back against the corner post of the champa. Conscious thought began to slip away into the well of darkness. As she fell down that well, she reached out to the baby she was losing and weakly hoped that they would both be dead before the dogs or the zopilotes found them.

# CHAPTER THREE

Has the rain a father? Or who has begotten the
drops of dew...?

Job 38:28

The cow with a crooked horn was born under a
wandering star. She was not a bad sort really, in her
heart. She was, in fact, the best of the seven cows
that Don Nando owned. For one thing, during the
seven months each year in which she produced milk,
she routinely gave about seven liters per day, which
was better than average for her mixed Brahma/Jersey
kind. She was also even tempered. She generally had
good sense. She didn't run. She didn't kick. She just
loved to wander.

Catcho Pando they called her in Catracho Spanish because of her crooked horn. Catcho Pando loved
to wander. Around midnight on this particular night,
she awoke for no particular reason. The others stood
sleeping in the drizzle or chewed the cud slowly in

a dreamy daze. But Catcho Pando couldn't sleep, and she couldn't stand to just stand there. She wasn't hungry or thirsty. She was just ... restless.

She followed her restlessness across the corral and through the gate and up the lane to the mango tree field. She felt as if she were looking for something out there in the night. She crossed the field in the drizzling dark, as if she had somewhere in particular to go ... which, of course, she didn't. So, for reasons known only to God and a wandering cow, she proceeded in a direct line to the far corner of the field where there was a barbed-wire gate. The local name for such a gate, as you might recall, is a *falso*. Catcho Pando peered through the falso into the dark lane on the other side and scratched her head on the free post. The falso had not been used in at least five months, and the termites had left only the husk of the free-hanging posts before they had headed off down the cellulose trail for parts unknown. With the first push of her crooked-horned head, the falso collapsed, leaving this wandering cow standing stock still in surprise.

While it is true that most cows won't willingly go through an unfamiliar opening in the dark, Catcho Pando was not like most cows in this regard. Despite the dark and the rain, and the lack of any particular reason to do so, a wandering cow, when presented with an unexpectedly open gate, will pass through it almost every time. In keeping with her particular kind, after getting over her startle, Catcho Pando lumbered forward again, as if she knew where she was going.

Passing through the gate, she actually had two choices in that direction. Don Nando, who had made this particular gate, was known both for being inventive and for being tight with his money. When the country people who knew him said, "You know Don Nando," they would wink while their left hand held their right elbow, the sign of a penny pincher. That was true. Yet everyone who knew him also admired him for being both smart and industrious, ingenious particularly for doing two things well for the price of doing one thing. Nando had made this particular gate with two loops and a free post on either end so that the gate could swing from both sides of the opening. It actually served to control three openings, depending upon which direction it was swung. Before it had collapsed, it had closed off the mango field. When opened on the right and swung to the left, it gave access to Nando's *milpa*, his "cornfield," which had been harvested a month before the rains began the previous October. When opened from the left and swung in to the right, it gave access to Señora Ondina Aleman's old pasture, which Nando sometimes rented. Since no one else ever did and she no longer had a cow in the pasture or a house on the other side of it, Nando's "three gates for the price of one" arrangement served him well ... termites and wandering cows notwithstanding.

By the time Catcho Pando was halfway through the gate, the thought of exploring the milpa was beginning to take form in her contrary head. "Didn't the man have corn growing over here?" she asked herself. "That would be worth looking into ... " But just then, for purposes of His own and in ways known only to Him, the God of the heavens continued to gently but surely guide this wandering cow. Just as her head began to sway toward the cornfield on the right, a raindrop ... a particular raindrop ... a guiding raindrop, landed directly in the absolute dead center of Catcho Pando's left eye. Her first reaction was just what you or I would have done. She flinched, blinked, and shut her left eye hard, turning her head to the left. But then, unlike what you or I would do, but just as every other cow would do, she followed the law of the quadruped. Since in motion, she continued in the direction her head had turned toward. She walked on through the left-hand gate and up into the overgrown old pasture.

Once she was committed to the old cow path that meandered up into the overgrown pasture, Catcho Pando, still true to her kind, quickly forgot her plans from a moment before. She no more thought of exploring the milpa than you might recall your quickly fading dream from the night before. Both eyes fixed ahead, both ears forward, she tentatively but steadily ascended the path. She began wondering, *Doesn't this path lead to the old milking champa?*

Now that particular raindrop that had landed dead center in Catcho Pando's left eye did not just fall there by chance. No, it was a guiding raindrop. It was the guiding raindrop chosen by God the instant when Magdalena finally asked for help. But it took a little while to bring it to bear. That special raindrop had been born seventeen minutes earlier, thirteen thousand feet above the shoals over the mouth of the Rio Esteban. There, in a winter *chubasco* or massive storm like this one, the relatively warm, humid air rising from the Caribbean littoral stacks up against the cooler air cycling down from the Cordillera Nombre de Dios. Pushed higher and higher by the immense engine of the warm tropical sea, the uppermost reaches of the storm clouds flowed to the top of the troposphere, along the boundary of atmosphere in which we live and the stratosphere, devoid of life. It chills the upper troposphere to eighty-five to one hundred degrees below zero Fahrenheit. There, between the burning stars and the crenellations of the coastal palisades, suspended water molecules facing these frigid temperatures instantly cool and condense and begin to coalesce in crystalline associations.

The initial components of the seed crystals comprise only a few molecules, but in the still, pregnant air just outside the jet stream, they rapidly gather-in more slow-moving siblings. Once a critical mass of water molecules in crystalline array is formed, the pull of gravity on the accumulated mass of the tiny crystal overcomes the relatively weak attraction offered by the surrounding molecules in the thin atmosphere.

A droplet, less than two-tenths of a millimeter in diameter, is set for the fall.

But, just before the initial acceleration, in the poise before the fall, something happens within the framework of this particular raindrop, the *guiding* raindrop. An electron in one of the paired hydrogen atoms is chosen and actualized in an extreme hybrid orbital: one of the nearly infinite number of possible orbitals, but one that cost God a lot in the rebalancing of Avagadro's number of other realized and potential electron orbitals consequently effected throughout the storm system. As a result of this chosen orbital, the hydrogen couplet is oriented so as to optimize a bonding to a specific passing ionized oxygen atom. The interaction of these three atoms affects the next nodal event, or interaction of particles, beginning a chain of consequences that result in a specific vector and acceleration. The seed is sown. It is cast in a particular direction and begins the fall toward the earth.

As the droplet begins the fall, it collides with other water molecules lower in the cloud mass and gathers them in like a rolling snowball. It gains mass and acceleration, forming a falling nucleus for other droplets. A falling triple star becomes a hurtling galaxy of oxygen and hydrogen. When the falling rain nucleus reaches a specific mass, perhaps twenty-five times the original seed, the weak ties that hold it together can no longer withstand the collisions with other gas particles in the shifting thermal currents. It falls apart. It fragments into twenty-five new rain droplets, seeds for a gathering family, then a gathering host that falls together, then changes direction in synchrony, then falls together again, like a school of silver fish flashing in the darkness, all flying pell-mell together toward their appointment with the earth.

All of this, all of these shooting stars and bright brigades and schools of silent siblings, all of these billions times billions of interactions must be perfectly choreographed in God's grand ballet of the storm. But our particular raindrop, the guiding raindrop, had required prescient selection and direction and then a subatomic reordering of the entire immense storm system as ordained by its new future permutations. And all of this to guide a raindrop to guide a cow who promptly forgot the splash and very soon forgot the change in plans.

The wandering cow with the crooked horn may have forgotten, within a few blinks, the raindrop that landed in her eye, that turned her head, that set her onto the path, that crossed an overgrown pasture to an old milking champa. But God did not forget the steering raindrop ... not ever ... not for eternity.

Imagine that God really is who He is supposed to be. Imagine that He really is omniscient. That's a lot to know. For instance, consider what there is to know about this one storm over a wild and forgotten backwater of one small country of one small subcontinent of this one planet. The clouds of Honduras's north coast winter storms are deep type-three maritime systems that extend from the sullen Caribbean Sea to the frigid upper reaches of the troposphere, six thousand meters, nearly four miles above the muddy path, and are often hundreds of miles in diameter.

Just in tonight's storm there are billions of tons of water suspended in the air in droplets of less than half a millimeter in diameter, trillions upon trillions of those droplets. These droplets themselves and the atmosphere in which they are suspended make up galaxies of blazing suns of hydrogen and oxygen, and nitrogen, rogue-star free radicals, expanding nebulae of inert gases, giant paired suns of sulfur oxide, and gravity wells of suspended heavy metals, all separated by immense empty spaces...empty of everything...everything except the presence of the knowledge of God.

The knowledge and understanding that human-kind has come to regarding the makeup and behavior of things on this level at the very fabric of existence cannot, I suppose, even be compared to the knowledge of an omniscient God's. The differences are too vast to bear any substantive comparison. But some of our greatest minds' greatest insights into how matter and energy behave and are held together on this level of quantum mechanics sometimes give glimpses into the awesome workings of God's mind. According to our best understanding of the laws governing subatomic physical interactions, every indivisible particle and quantum of energy that comprises both these smaller universes and the larger ones that they constitute...every individual indivisible component exists in "a coherent superposition of all the possible states permitted by its wave function." That is, every subatomic particle exists, at any given instant, in an almost infinite number of potential directions, positions, and velocities. Every particle actually exists in all places at the same time, travels in all vectors at the same time. It is only when that particle is observed that the potential parameters become actual.

Heisenberg's brilliant leap of reasoning about position and velocity uncertainty, and Schrödinger's elegant mathematical description of electron wave states, Einstein, Podolsky, and Rosen's paradox, and John Stewart Bell's Inequality Principle all give glimpses of a universe that is ultimately defined by an observer, a knower. In the absence of an observer for every particle or quanta's position and interaction, that particle, and the universe to which it belongs, theoretically remains in superposition ... an infinite number of potential universes that can only exist if known.

Nonetheless, this one universe exists. These particles that constitute air and water, blood and bone, mud and stone, all of the innumerable, incalculable weight of them, actually exist. You are you, and you are actually reading this book. Yet the position velocity, mass, direction, and interaction of every sub-atomic particle and quanta that comprises you and this book mathematically require a knower to exist.

Imagine that the knower is God.

Imagine one step further. Imagine that he chose the raindrop. This is not too much of a stretch, not too much of a stretch for the observer to choose. It is, in fact, a direct permutation of Schrödinger's equation. It is the working solution to the Einstein, Podolsky, Rosen paradox. By choosing the locus of a particular electron orbital for observation, for instance, the moment the electron is observed there, it is determined. And all of the infinite possibilities of its location coalesce as the potential becomes actual.

It is not too much of a stretch for the observer to determine ... to choose. But it is a great risk. For every choice has a consequence. It negates all other possibilities. And every consequence changes all future possibilities. The choice of one axis of polarity on one charged particle in one water droplet potentially affects all others in the storm system.

> For want of a nail the shoe was lost.
> For want of the shoe the horse was lost.
> For want of the horse the rider was lost.
> For want of the rider the battle was lost.

Our grandparents' grandparents knew some form of that *dicho*, that aphorism that reminded them that great consequences may turn on a small point. The cumulative outcome of one such small choice for one raindrop in one storm might bring about a future climactic shift, or a madman to come to power, a beloved to be lost, or a great talent never to be born or ... What if the outcome of one misplaced choice causes the entire experienced universe to come apart at the seams?

There is a lot to know and a lot to consider and great risk to be taken when choosing a raindrop to save a lost and dying woman, about whose existence not another soul in the universe cares. But Holy

Scripture instructs us that in all these things and more God works "oftentimes with man to bring his soul from the pit to be enlightened with the light of the living."

To all outward appearances, Catcho Pando was not too interested in the Heisenberg Uncertainty Principle. She was not even overly concerned with the concept that God's intervention, even on the smallest level, requires a comprehensive reordering of the possibilities of the *new* universe that results. She steadily ascended the hill in the dark hour before dawn, dipping and swaying from side to side, pausing occasionally to snatch a bite of *secate* or *crespia*. She never once wondered why she had turned in this direction. She may have thought a little hazily about what she would find at the top of the hill, though I doubt she ever imagined she might find a dying young woman on the floor of the old champa. She might have even wondered how she would get home, but she never once wondered why. Humans are the creatures who wonder why. Cows don't. There are no mysteries for cows. Yet this mystery of the turning of a raindrop is important to humans. It is important to the story. As you will see, it was important to Magdalena. And it is important to the rest of us out here *en el medio de quien sabe donde.* For while on occasion God may push aside obstacles for us like the Red Sea, and sometimes he might guide with a pillar of fire by night. Out here in Colón, it seems, He mostly uses the raindrop method.

# CHAPTER FOUR

How much more those who dwell in houses of clay,
Whose foundation is in the dust, Who are crushed
before the moth!

Job 4:19

Don Nando not only had seven cows; he also had
seven children. Well, at one time he had seven children. Somehow, he kept forgetting that Adolfo, his
oldest, was no longer counted among the living on
this earth. This May would make two years since he
died while diving for conch on a rig out of Puerto
Lempira. Dying at sea as he had, there had been no
body brought home, no proper *velorio*, no "wake."
There had been no digging of the grave, no funeral
service. No grave to keep chopped and clean. Somehow, it just never seemed real. Nando always felt in
the back of his mind that Adolfo was still nearby, just
around the corner. That he would be back soon. He
would have been nineteen now.

Ramon was Nando's second son, and he would soon complete his eighteenth year. Ramon was gone now too, nearly nine months gone. Ramon had always been close to Adolfo … looked up to him. Adolfo's death had left Ramon kind of hollow and anchorless. On the first anniversary of Adolfo's death, Ramon had just disappeared. Three months passed before they received a message from the Hondutel office in Balfate. Ramon had called and left a message with the Hondutel radiophone operator. He was all right and working on a shrimp trawler out of Isla Mujeres. He had called again three months later and said he missed them and was planning to send his next paycheck. That was a few months ago.

Just yesterday, Nando's brother-in-law, Julio Vicente Ortiz Ponce, came out from La Ceiba, showing off his new Toyota Hilux. Julio was the oldest son of Ramon Ortiz, Doña Mirian's father. The old man, Don Ramon, was a Columbian by birth and disagreeable by nature. Nando had always called the old man (outside the old man's hearing) El Columbiano. Everyone said that Julio, Don Ramon's only son, was *hecho de la misma tela,* "cut from the same cloth," just like him. When the old man died, Nando (who had never liked either of them) took to calling Julio "El Columbiano" too. When El Columbiano came out visiting, expecting to show off his new truck, to be well fed, and to spend the night in Mirian and Nando's bed, he also brought a package with a note from Ramon and a money order for what to Nando seemed like a great deal of money … enough to buy another cow. Ramon had gone *mojado* (wetback), and was in Houston, Texas. He was lonesome, but he had a job in construction that was paying well. He had sent some money through his Uncle Julio (who had a street address and a telephone for the money order to arrive in La Ceiba).

Nando smiled to himself that Ramon had shown some sense by both writing the amount he was sending in the letter and by sending it as a money order instead of cash. He must understand his uncle Julio well. Still chuckling, Nando went to let his beloved Mirian know that they had news from their Ramon ... and that he was going to kill a chicken; El Columbiano was visiting.

After Adolfo's death, Doña Mirian seemed to wander off for a while too. At first, like Ramon, her second son, she couldn't eat or sleep. But life went on. And, like someone who survives a traumatic amputation, she recovered, broken and mended, weakened and changed; yet life went on. Mirian, beautiful and strong, vibrant and confident, had lost her first-born baby. She limped on into life, suddenly aged and diminished. But she had other babies, and they needed her. She brought in her fences and applied her energy to her babies: Mári, Mona, and Rosalia. Rosalia was really not a baby any longer. She was nine years now. She was the fifth of the seven children. Her mind, her hands, and her tongue, like her mother's, were naturally quick and strong. Yet ever since a crippling fever when she was two years of age, her legs never grew strong. Her feet were weak and bent inward. Rosalia could move around the yard and house with agility on her crutches (or when no one was watching, on her hands). But, there were many tasks she couldn't help with and some that she needed help with.

Mári was the youngest child, the seventh of seven. She was Mirian's *tierna,* her "tender one," her baby. She was five, fast, and funny. She was also what in English you'd call "a pistol," "strong willed," or just "hardheaded." In the campo, she was called a *burrita,* a "little burro." You get the picture. She knew what she wanted and was usually in motion to get it. But sometimes when she was tired or when she was sick and particularly at the end of the day when she was sleeping ... she was still just five. With her long eyelashes resting on her soft cheeks, she was ... "the tender little one," the *tiernita.*

Ramona Liset Zuniga Ortiz, *Mona,* was the second to the youngest, the sixth out of seven. She was the first girl named *a fuera de los padres,* "beyond the names of the parents' parents," since, of course, Adolfo, Ramon, Elizabet, and Rosalia were named for the paternal and maternal grandfathers and grandmothers in order. But Mona was named by Doña Mirian for two childhood girlfriends. Mirian loved her girlfriends. Liset still lived nearby. And Ramona, Mirian's second cousin, was born on the same day as Mirian. Closer than a sister, Ramona had died in childbirth ten years ago. Though Mirian alone had named Ramona Liset, she alone, for reasons of her own, always called Mona "*Angelita.*"

Mona, born with Down's syndrome, was Doña Mirian's little angel. Mirian knew that Mona, her "Angelita", like Rosalia, would be Mirian's baby after all the other children had babies of their own.

Elizabet, the oldest girl, the third of seven, was fifteen years old...fifteen going on forty. Mirian sometimes thought that her Elizabet had been born going on forty. She was quiet and serious and always had been. Elizabet was entering her *terser curso en basico* (essentially the ninth grade) and was determined to finish her *bachillerato en comercio* (a high school degree in business). In order to do that, she would have to ride her bicycle six miles each way to the *colegio,* the "high school" in Balfate, the only colegio between Jutiapa and Rio Esteban.

Elizabet was the kind of person who never raised her voice, stayed on task, and rarely looked for attention. She was the kind of person that, though you hadn't noticed at the time, when you looked back, you remembered that she had been there too. She was the kind of person that, without that kind of person, the human race would soon grind to a halt.

Finally, there was Arturo... *el de en medio.* Three children older, three children younger, Arturo was the middle child. He was always in the middle: in the middle of his sixth grade class, at twelve years old halfway between Elizabet and Rosalia, of average build, and of an agreeable, though not extreme, disposition, Arturo was the peacemaker between siblings, the messenger between parents and, among his friends, the middle of the pick, but always included. He was … well, *el medio.*

So then, you have Don Nando and Doña Mirian, Adolfo, Ramon, Elizabet, Arturo, Rosalia, Mona, Mári, and Uncle Julio (El Columbiano). On first pass the myriad of personalities and names and relationships can make one's head spin. And this is a nearly intact nuclear family. After a couple of spouses have passed on or run off, or married cousins and all had children, trying to sort these matters out can make everything spin. For now though, the story centers on Arturo, the middle child.

Arturo, by nature, had a strong tendency to follow set plans and patterns. By dent of an active and curious mind, he had a habit of constantly questioning his own plans and patterns. Arturo awoke at half past four every morning. This morning at half past four, he awoke and wondered, *Why don't I just stay in bed for an hour? School won't start again for three weeks, so I don't have to worry about getting the milking done before school. I could stay in bed for an hour and still get it done before the lecheros pass.* This is what Arturo thought every morning when school was out for the winter rainy season, *la temporada de lluvias.* But this morning, like every morning, within five minutes of half past four, Arturo's bare feet touched the concrete floor. He stood up and walked through thick darkness to the door. Through the door, he turned right, five steps down the covered porch to the *llave,* "the water spigot" with its bucket at the end of the porch.

As he splashed his face and hair, he thought, *Why*

*wash? I'll soon be wet all through in this rain.* Then, *Why dry? I'll soon be wet again,* he thought while he reached for the towel on the nail.

Arturo hitched up his pants, buttoned up his shirt, and pulled his rubber boots on over his bare feet. It was nearly five a.m. now, *el fin de la madrugada.* The dawn would be here soon. He stared out into the deepest purple of the first turning toward morning, out across the *solár,* the backyard, and into the corral. He looked hard into the near darkness for several minutes then dropped his head and stepping out into the drizzle. He muttered *"caray!"* under his breath. Now, *caray* is not a very strong expletive, more like an exclamation like *"dang"* or *"Ai Chihuahua".* Being twelve years old and having grown up in the campo, Arturo, of course, knew worse words. But being Doña Mirian's son, he just never used those words.

*Caray* is what Arturo's papi, Don Nando, said when he had to go looking for Catcho Pando. And that is what Arturo knew he had to do now, look for Catcho Pando. He could see only six cows standing together in the corral. That meant that the crooked horned cow must be off wandering. Arturo stooped and straddled and ducked through between the second and third rail of the corral fence. He always climbed through this section between the second and third rail, though he often wondered why he didn't just use the gate. He strode alongside, then behind and beyond the sleepy cud clatch of standing cattle. He most certainly counted them again.

But, sure enough, one was missing. He closed the gate between the corral and the lane to the paddock beyond. At least he would make sure that the six stayed up close for milking while he went to look for the Catcho Pando ... for the third time in a week. *Caray!*

Arturo's eyes were completely adjusted to the dark. Since awakening, he had not even seen a candle. In the open solar and corral therefore, he could make out shapes and obstacles, even beneath this cloud over. But he knew that the sunken lane from the back of the paddock to the mango field would be as black as the jungle at night. He doubted that Catcho Pando would be standing by herself down in the dark lane. She generally followed any track to its end. But if she were standing in the lane, he'd run right into her before he saw her. So anyway, anyone knows that you can't walk in the jungle at night. Instead, Arturo cut across to the lower end of the paddock. That's where she'd been three nights ago. He bet that his Papi had left the gate from the head of the lane into the paddock open and that wandering cow just couldn't resist.

But no, not this morning. He never could predict that crooked-horned cow. Arturo cautiously tramped a wide swath through the entire paddock and found nothing bigger than two stray hens sleeping in the avocado tree. He ducked through the fence into the mango field. Again, he began a wide swath. He had not completed half the arc through the mango field before being brought up short by a deeply petulant cow calling out into the early morning drizzle. *That came from beyond the Mango field; off to the left and up the hill. She must be up the hill in the old champa of Doña Ondina.* Like whistling in the dark, he heard her calling out a second time, bawling "Anybody there?"

Arturo walked straight toward the corner gate, head down and tucked in between his shoulders. He wiped the rain off his face. When he reached the corner, he could see at a glance what had happened. The morning was coming on and the air more blue than purple now. He could see the collapsed gate, the fresh, deep hoof prints in the mud, now filled with coffee-colored water. He wondered for a moment why that crazy old cow had turned up into the over-grown pasture of Doña Ondina's instead of into his Papi's cornfield. Then, shaking his dripping head, he jumped the worst of the mud in the gate crossing and followed the way Catcho Pando had gone, uphill toward the old champa.

As Arturo followed the overgrown path, he won-dered why he kept dodging the highest of the waist-high brush hanging into the path. After all, he was already soaked clear through. He mumbled words to that effect as he dodged the next one anyway. As he climbed the hill, he began to think about what was at the end of the path.

When he was little, the *casaria,* the household on top of the hill, had been inhabited with a large and constantly changing cast of loosely related chil-dren, barely cared for by a tired old abuelita, Doña

Ondina Aleman. Doña Ondina, he'd heard, had gotten sick and moved to La Ceiba the month before his sixth birthday. The children all scattered, presumably farmed out to even more distant relations. Or maybe, the older ones found work somewhere. Arturo remembered that they were poor. His mother Doña Mirian always said, "Poor is how you think." Arturo didn't know how those kids thought, but he always thought of this homestead on top of the hill as "Where those poor kids lived." Poor though they were, the place sure was livelier then.

No one had lived there for eight years now. The buildings had all fallen in except for the champa. Arturo's papi had put a new *manaca* (palm thatch) roof on the champa when Arturo was seven. Don Nando was renting the pasture then, and part of the rent was paid by putting a roof on the champa. They hadn't kept cattle in this pasture for more than a year now, and the manaca would be about two years past its usefulness. Arturo hardly ever went up there. It was kind of creepy. Where there had once been so much activity, now it was all silent and fallen in. It felt like … like someone was waiting or watching. Well, he had to go up there now. He had just heard that crazy Catcho Pando bellowing from up there … three times now.

*Ay Caray!*

When Arturo got to the top of the hill, the gray dawn was coming on. He was soaked to the skin (despite dodging all the highest bushes). He was scratched and muddy, and he was in no mood to spend time looking around. He just wanted to put a lasso on that Catcho Pando, get back home, and get the milking done. He ducked under the dripping eaves of the champa and squinted into the darker blue and musty air. There she was standing right in front of him, right in the middle of the champa, looking right back at him. She ducked and shook her head then murmooed as if to say, "What took you so long?" As his eyes adjusted to the dim light in the old champa, Arturo, speaking softly, headed for Catcho Pando (with the rope held behind his back). She patiently stood staring forward while Arturo stepped up beside her. She exhaled a heavy breath smelling of wild *albaca* and wet *crespia,* but she still didn't move as Arturo ran the lasso around her steaming neck.

Arturo turned and started out walking, but when he got to the end of the rope, he was pulled up short. Catcho Pando had her feet set and didn't budge. He went back, pushed her head sideways, got her to shift her weight, and tried again. But … nope … nada, "*No lo cede.*" "Not gonna budge."

That's when Arturo saw it. The muddy old pile of rags on the far edge of the champa moved. Arturo froze. It moaned and coughed. If he could have, he would have jumped right out of his skin. *Ay Caray !*

# CHAPTER FIVE

Who does great things unfathomable, and won-
drous works without number. Were He to pass me
by I would not see Him; Were He to move past me,
I would not perceive Him.

Job 9:10–11

Death should come as no surprise for one born and
raised out here in the *campo*. Most have been exposed
to the death of livestock as a matter of routine on
a farm. Many have seen far too much of the death
of loved ones far too early in life. Arturo remembered the *velorio* (the wake) of three of his four
grandparents. At nine years of age, he had helped
dig the grave of a first cousin. At ten, he had helped
Elizabet sort out and put away the few things the
boat captain had sent after his oldest brother's death.
His parents and Ramon had been still too shaken to
deal with it. Death in the *campo* still held a degree
of fear and fascination. But its face was recogniz-

able, an accepted part of *la lucha*, "the struggle" of this life. Now death might be one thing, but a pile of rags moving and moaning when you're all alone at the end of the night in a creepy falling down, old champa is another thing altogether. Thinking back on that encounter, Arturo never could remember the subconscious jump and 180-degree twist in the air, hitting the ground running with the lasso lead rope still clutched in his hand. He didn't remember running "devil take the hindmost" for the far side of the champa. He just remembered being jerked off his feet, his arm nearly pulled out of his shoulder socket when he was brought up short at the end of the lasso. One end was wound round and firmly clinched in his right hand. The other end was tied around the neck of an immovable object: Catcho Pando. Feet planted, knees locked, chin tucked, and neck stiff, she just wasn't going to be moved from this spot … not in that direction … not yet.

Feet flying out into the air, Arturo landed hard on his tailbone. His teeth clacked together too late to catch the wind knocked out of him. By the time he finally found his next breath, his head had begun to clear of the blind white terror. The pile of rags on the far edge of the champa coughed. *Rags don't cough*, Arturo thought. *Duendes* (ghosts) *don't either, I think. And, duendes don't stink*, he thought. *At least they shouldn't stink like this. But don't go over there. You don't need to know. You just need to get that crazy cow out of here and back home and milked.*

While Arturo was thinking this, his contrary feet

were walking over to that stinking, coughing pile of rags. *Don't look at it,* he thought while his unblinking contrary eyes strained to see if it moved. Arturo stood over the body as the blue-gray dawn illuminated what was left of Magdalena. She looked dead. She very nearly was. But the spirit of God who had sat with the young girl while she waited for her mother, the person who stood close by the broken woman at the mirror, the one who set guard over her on the park bench ... he waited still. He had turned a raindrop and rebalanced the storm, just to turn the head of a wandering cow to bring a young boy, scared stiff and soaked to the skin, to the place where she lay dying. That unlikely rescuer now stood over her, looking down, dripping and shivering. He swallowed hard and then wondered how long it had been since he had forgotten to breathe out or to breathe in.

After lying still a long while, Magdalena finally caught a ragged breath. Still looking down at this body in rags, Arturo finally remembered to let his breath out, with one long emphatic *Aayy hombre!* Catcho Pando shook her head. Slobber flew. Somehow it seemed she knew that now that this meeting had taken place, it was time to go. She eyed the rope in Arturo's hand and started walking for the house. Slipping and skipping down the muddy path, trying to catch up and keep up with the now trotting cow, Arturo was dragged through the wet bushes down the hill. Trying to regain the lead and a measure of his badly bruised twelve-year-old dignity was a challenge for Arturo that he didn't completely accomplish until they were through the gate and halfway across the mango tree field. He was running as fast as he could in rain-filled rubber boots, but his thoughts ran faster. Almost all of his thoughts were questions. *Who is that really sick woman lying in the mud? How did she get there? What happened to her? Is she going to die? Has she died already?*

He thought up a lot more questions while trotting back the muddy lane with that crazy cow. But the only question that he found any answer to was "What should I do?" The answer to that came easily. He had to tell, his papi, Don Nando, and his mami, Doña Mirian. They would know what to do. Straight up the sunken lane they ran, the trotting cow and her boy in tow. In the corral, Arturo let go of the rope and half running, half sliding, he steered for the section right next to the gate, aimed for the space between the second and third rail, and dove through. Nando was already up of course. He had heard Arturo go out after Catcho Pando and was now in the galera, milking the second cow. He saw Arturo come sliding in with her, run right past him across the corral, and dive through the slats on the far side of the fence.

"Turo! What are you doing? I'm over here." Arturo immediately locked up the brakes, slid to a stop in the *solár,* turned 180 degrees in midslide, reversed engines, and dove back through between the second and third rail. *Why can't that boy just use the gate?* Nando thought.

Most Hondurans in general, and those who grew up in the campo in particular, tend to *andar lijero.*

They walk lightly and carefully. They don't make much sound, don't splash much, and don't get their clothes all messy and muddy. Even traveling down a muddy road or across a mucky corral, one is likely to stay remarkably clean. North Americans do seem to stamp and slip and splash around a lot more. They are privately considered to be *descuidado*, or "reckless." Arturo was, of course, *catracho*, or *puro Indio* as they say, "born to the countryside." When Arturo stomped and slipped and splashed a muddy trail across the corral on a beeline to where Nando was just finishing with the second cow Don Nando raised one eyebrow and thought, *Well, I suppose he is going to make thirteen soon.*

While Artruo was performing his impromptu vaudeville act across the corral, Mona had been carrying a bucket of water and a clean towel from her mami to her papi. With it, he would wash and dry his hands and then the udder of the last cow to milk, Catcho Pando. Mona had concentrated on doing the task carefully. When her papi took the towel and smiled down at her with a wink, she knew she had done it all well. Her face, which had been drawn down hard in a frown of concentration, lit up like the sun coming suddenly from behind a cloud.

This is how they were standing, like judge and joyful little jury, when Arturo splashed to a stop to testify breathlessly before them. "I was up at the old champa, Doña Ondina's I mean, looking for that crazy cow, the Catcho Pando. She was up there, and she wouldn't leave until I saw her ... the dead woman,

I mean. Well, I don't think she's dead yet, just very sick, but she wouldn't leave ... Catcho Pando wouldn't leave I mean, until I saw her. And, I think she's, well, you know, *impreñada ... encinta* I mean, the woman I mean ... the dead woman ... *Caray!*

Arturo's testimony had come out all a' jumble, all in one breath, and not nearly as he'd meant. It's hard to explain such things as unexpectedly finding a dying pregnant woman in an abandoned champa in the early morning light at any age. Then the urgency of the situation coupled with Arturo's twelve-year-old embarrassment over how to tell his father the pregnant part just did him in. He knew that a cow would be *impreñada*. He'd heard other people talk in odd ways about a girl being *embarasada*. And his mother, Doña Mirian, only ever referred to the condition as the Bible did, *encinta,* "with child." So what was he supposed to say?

Altogether, he felt as if he'd bungled his report. When he looked up at judge and jury reflecting the same bewildered expressions to each other, he knew that he had. Then Mona did what she often did when not sure what to do. She laughed. That seemed to get them all past this false start and gave Arturo a chance to take a deep breath and try again. "Papi, listen. I went looking for Catcho Pando about an hour ago. I found her up at the old champa of Doña Ondina. When I tried to lead her back, at first she balked and wouldn't come. Then I found a woman there. I don't know who she is. She might be dead, but I don't think so. She must be very sick. She is lying in the mud, and she doesn't move. But she coughed, and I think I saw her breathe. What are we going to do?"

You might notice that Arturo avoided the pregnant part altogether in his second report. He wasn't going back to that subject. *"No vale la pena."* "Just not worth it." he thought.

Nando answered as he usually answered the question, "What are we going to do?" He answered it of course, by doing the next right thing. He didn't say a word. But he stood and hung the towel that Mona had brought on its nail on the post. He put the water bucket at the base of the same post beside the milk bucket. He tied Catcho Pando up short and snug to the next post in the galera, swooped down, caught up Mona, and carried her giggling back to the house.

Nando put Mona down inside the kitchen door and gave Mirian a brief sketch of what Arturo had told him. She didn't question or argue. She could see that he had a plan in mind. She offered to finish the milking and suggested Rosalia watch Mona and Mari. Nando nodded and, turning, called Elizabet to follow him. Elizabet came without questioning or complaining. She knew that when her father used that tone he had a reason. She caught up at the edge of the corral, and they entered together. (They used the gate.)

Arturo was waiting in the galera, uneasily shifting his weight from foot to foot. Don Nando picked up his machete from where it was resting on top of the half wall that ran across the back of the galera. He turned to Elizabet and said, "Arturo found a sick woman up in Ondina's champa. We'll have to carry her down. You bring two sacks from the bodega. Arturo, bring some *alambre de amare* (tie wire). There's about half a pound on the post under the *guanabana* tree. We'll meet at the head of the lane."

Nando turned and walked out the eastern end of the galera. From the fenceline at the upper end of the paddock, he cut two stout *madreado* branches. By the time he had finished trimming and cleaning them, Elizabet was there with the feedsacks, and Arturo brought the wire. Nando put the poles on his left shoulder, picked up the machete in his right hand, and headed off across the paddock.

Arturo and Elizabet regained the last ten yards to catch up with Don Nando at the lower corner of the mango field. He was standing there looking at the opened gap, machete stuck in the mud by his right boot. He was pulling on his right ear as he often did when deep in thought. He took in the termite ruined prop poles of the falso lying in the mud. By both nature and nurture, Nando was a tracker. Unlike many men of his generation and background, he could read simple printed words and signs. He could even read the Bible with some effort. But he could read the signs left by the passage of man or beast as you can read this book. Now he considered the cow prints filled with still muddy water. The tracks started off heading straight toward and then veered abruptly away from last autumn's milpa (cornfield). The tracks turned instead toward Doña Ondina's overgrown *potrero*. With his hand on his chin, he shook his head and said to himself and the still morning air, *"Que raro,"* "how strange."

The direction Catcho Pando had chosen wasn't what you'd expect from your average cow, that's true, but Nando had come to anticipate she'd choose the unexpected. But seeing the tracks that began to head toward the milpa, where most cows would go, but then swerved away to where most cows wouldn't be interested put Nando into a pensive mood.

While looking over the muddy tracks in the gate and wondering at the tale they told, Nando's eyes came to rest on a track in the middle of the way. There was nothing to distinguish this one *huella*, this hoofprint from the other cow-hoof-shaped lakelets. Yet, as his eyes rested on that one, for a moment he dreamed. He dreamed of singing stars in a cobalt sky. He dreamed of crushing cold above a world of storm and the breathless wait before the drop. He dreamed of falling, falling past mountaintops, of stunning speed and disintegrating collisions ... and a school of silver fish. He dreamed all this in the span of a few heartbeats. Then he shivered and looked up and thought, *Someone was walking on my grave.*

Elizabet had caught up to stand beside her father on his left. She followed his eyes and saw only mud. But she felt something strange. Like her father, for an instant, she felt that sense of "otherness," that the Greeks called *numenos,* that slight but distinct residue of holiness left in a raindrop so recently touched by the finger of God. She glanced up at Nando, who stared an instant longer, then blinked his eyes and shook his head. As for Elizabet, the practical one, her thoughts turned quickly to a question of whether this uncharacteristic woolgathering of her father's might be the first sign of senility. She'd seen her grandmother go that way. One day she was dreamy like that, and the next day she put her dress on backwards ... and a few months later, she wouldn't get out of bed. *Is that the way it's going to be with Papi?* she thought. *And who will take care of all of us then? I just know it will end up being me.* Not that any of these worries happened, of course. Don Nando lived another thirty years and was by no means senile on his last day. That's just Elizabet.

Arturo had come up to stand behind his father on the right. For a few seconds, he too was caught up in the scene of seeing other things. And for a half an instant, he too felt a slight something fearful passing nearby. But, as you must remember, Arturo had already been through a lot that morning. Having already jumped out of and then climbed back into his skin several times that morning, he was somewhat inoculated against a sense of wonder in a muddy cow print. So, his next thought was *I'm hungry,* then, *Why are we standing here? We need to get her to the house and see when breakfast will be.*

They all three came to the same conclusion at about the same time. Rousing and turning to the left, first Nando, then Elizabet, then Arturo passed through the gate and into Ondina's overgrown pasture. Still, in passing through, they all three avoided the cow track in the middle of the lane. From that point forward, this strange business of the rescue became really rather work-a-day. The sun did throw a tentative ray through an opening in the dissipating storm. With a glancing blow, it lit the world all scarlet-silver and burnt sienna-gold. But the rescue team hardly noticed. They just trudged on up the hill without comment or change of pace.

Steeped in the practical ways of country things, of meeting tasks straight-on, they ducked into the shadow of the old champa and set the materials down. They did not go to look at the woman first. They could see at a glance that there was a body at the far edge of the champa. Clearly they would need some way to carry her out of here, whether she were alive or dead. So why look?

Working together under the few necessary directions from Don Nando, they first constructed an *andas*, "a stretcher." They bound the sacks to the two parallel poles using the *alambre*, the tie wire. When it was completed, Nando and Arturo carried it over and set it down next to the body. Elizabet knelt down and turned the woman's face up from the dirt. Magdalena coughed out a weak cough and pulled in a ragged breath. They all three looked down on this poor creature, and none recognized her. Nando pointed to the andas with his chin, and with no further communication, Nando and Elizabet swung her over onto the feedsack base. Nando and Arturo took up the Madreado poles. With no further ceremony, they ducked out of that dilapidated champa and stepped out into the dawn.

Down the hill, through the fallen gate, out into the mango field they walked in single file back toward the house. As they approached the lane, Arturo stumbled a little, slipping in the mud. In the jostling, Magdalena's arm slipped over the edge of the andas and dangled there. Elizabet, who had been walking behind her father, increased her pace a little to pass him and place the arm back inside the stretcher. Entering into the lane, she took Arturo's place carrying the poles at the front of the stretcher, Arturo opening and closing the gate.

In this way, they worked and walked together. They carried Magdalena up the lane, through the paddock, across the corral, and into the *solar*. They set her down in the corridor of the porch that ran across the back of the house. Doña Mirian was waiting for them with a bucket of clean water, a dry towel, and an extra blanket.

Mirian took in the contents of the stretcher with a glance and then looked up at Nando and Arturo. Because of the strength of her presence, it was often forgotten that she was physically quite small. She often forgot this herself. She realized just then that she was looking up at Arturo. He must have been growing when she wasn't watching him here lately. But now was not the time for such musing. "Carry her in to Elizabet's bed," was all she said to Nando and Arturo. Turning to Elizabet, she said, "I'll need your help."

As soon as they had deposited the body, muddy rags and all, on Elizabet's bed, without further ceremony, the menfolk beat a hasty retreat. They carried the stretcher with them, left it on the porch, then headed out across the corral to see if the milking had been finished, (which, of course, it had been). Both were glad to have gotten back, relatively unscathed, to the men's world of mud and rope, nails and lumber, from the women's world, where they were cleaning up that body.

There, in the little room of Elizabet (for Elizabet, now fifteen, had taken over Adolfo and Ramon's room), Mirian straightened and stood back for a moment's better look. She had been loosening and removing some of the filthy clothes from the body of the unconscious young woman. Mirian had washed the mud away from the face of indeterminate age, and leaned back for a better look. *I know this girl,* she thought. *This was one of the Alemans ... Ondina's nieta, her granddaughter.* She cleaned some more and thought, *This is the one who kept to herself so much. She played with Adolfo some, though she was older, but this was that shy one, always nursing some hurt it seemed. She ran off before she finished básico. Ran off with that fool of a one-eyed chele verdurero. What was her name?*

*Magdalena. Yes, Magdalena was her name. The poor little bird has returned to the nest and found it empty and fallen from the tree.* She washed the face and touched the cheek of this broken young woman and sighed. "Pobrecita."

# CHAPTER SIX

For man is born to trouble as the sparks fly upward, but as for me, I would seek God, and I would place my cause before God.

Job 5:7–8

Mirian had Elizabet help her get the dirty rag of a dress off of Magdalena. Then she sent Rosalia out to wash it, while Elizabet brought her an extra *falda*, her school uniform skirt. While Elizabet and Rosalia were out of the room, Mirian removed the underclothes and washed the body. Mirian was a woman of a deep personal faith, and as she washed she prayed. These prayers were not really coherent sentences. They were more like whispers of the heart and pleading and commiseration with her God for the hurt she saw evidenced as she washed the wasted body.

"*O Dios mio. Tócala Señor. Lo siento. Lo siento mucho, pobrecita. Ojalá mi Dios.*" and so on like that. What she saw as she washed was a story of misery

written on skin and bone: gang tattoos, scars, cigarette burns, broken ribs and collarbone. Mirian may
have been a country woman, but she was no one's
fool. She knew what a *diez y ocho* tattoo looked like
and guessed at what it meant on a woman. Beyond
all that, this woman was so thin and pale. Barely still
in this world she was. Magdalena was a little larger
in frame than Mirian, but despite being so obviously
late in pregnancy, she appeared to weigh less. Mirian called Elizabet for the dress, and together they
put the skirt on and fastened it up over the swollen
belly. Mirian brought out from a box a school shirt
of Ramon's. It was still just a bit too big for Arturo.
The extra fullness allowed them to button the shirt
over the tautly stretched belly.

Altogether the effect was a little unnerving.
With the baggy, short-sleeved shirt over the navy
blue skirt, lying there so still and pale, she looked
like a schoolgirl laid out for her *velorio,* her "wake."
Mirian left her there in the little room, walked down
the *corredor* to the kitchen door, and called to Arturo.

The milking had been finished before they
returned with Magdalena. Don Nando was just
now taking the milk down the *accesso,* the footpath
to the coast road, to leave it there for the *lechero* to
pick up. Soon the lechero, " the milkman," would be
passing by on his morning rounds. This left Arturo
*pendiente,* with no other responsibilities than to stay
nearby awaiting further orders. At Mirian's call from
just inside the kitchen door, Arturo hopped up from
just outside the kitchen door, " all at the ready." *a*

*la orden,* as they say, so quickly that it would have startled a lesser woman than Mirian. She of course did not blink or hesitate.

*Mi amor,* get on your bicycle. Ride down and catch your father. Tell him we will need to hire the lechero to take the young woman to the hospital." Arturo hopped on his bike and flew fast down the caminito to the "highway" as everyone called it. Though the "highway," like the caminito, was a road of dirt (mud at this end of the rainy season), it was the "highway" on the only scale that matters, the local scale of things.

Almost no sooner had Arturo left than Arturo returned. *Round trip, eight minutes,* he thought as he landed on the solar, chickens and leaves still settling from his return arc. Though he was generally careful with his bicycle, in the haste and urgency of the moment, he laid it down on its side on the hardpacked earth of the solar, the back wheel still spinning, tick, tick, ticking against cardboard noisemaker he had wired to the struts of the rear wheel. The chickens slowly regained their composure while heatedly protesting the impertinence and impropriety of the boy rushing around startling private citizens and so forth.

Arturo's out-of-breath report back to Mirian was that his papi, Don Nando, was already talking to the lechero, who today was "Alejandro the *trigeño* from *Rio Coco.*" The lechero was not so much an individual person as a brief job description ... a position, an office, if you will. He was the guy who drove the pickup truck to haul the farmer's milk in various-sized and -shaped milk containers from the farm to the nearest refrigerated storage building for the Leyde Dairy Company (or on other routes, the Dos Pinos Dairy Company)... and then brought the empty containers back to their respective places along his return route. There were currently three lecheros for Leyde's route between Rio Coco and Jutiapa, two regulars and an alternate to cover the 365 days a year that there would be warm milk waiting where the farmers' path meets the road. Today, the lechero was Alejandro. In the racial melting pot of the countryside in Honduras, trigueño is a commonly used distinction of a person of mixed racial lineage. Rio Coco is just where Alejandro lived at the end of the day. Thus he was "Alejandro the trigeño from Rio Coco." Alejandro was widely known and generally liked along the coast road from Jutiapa to Rio Coco. He was easygoing, uncommonly generous, and known to be scrupulously honest with measurements and payments and other business dealings. He was also known to be a Christian. And, unlike so many who claimed the name, Alejandro generally acted as a Christian is supposed to act.

While Arturo was delivering his report, Doña Mirian was placing and removing and replacing perfectly round corn tortillas on the iron griddle on the clay stove at the end of the porch. As she removed them, she stacked them quickly onto a hand towel in a small plastic basket. His duty done for the moment, Arturo stood watching, silently shifting his weight from side to side. Neither spoke, both absorbed in their own thoughts. Neither one was uncomfortable with the silence of the other.

The last of the tortillas was just being dropped into the little basket when Nando came stomping his rubber boots on the stone before he stepped up onto the clean concrete porch. He said, "Alejandro's waiting at 'the highway' to take the girl to the Hospital Loma de Luz. It will take forty lempiras in *combustible* (fuel). He can't pick up the milk as he goes since she'll take up most of the truck's paila, so he'll have to go there special and return to the route. He says that the fuel belongs to the company, so we'll have to cover it. But he sees carrying the girl to the hospital as his Christian obligation, so he'll split the cost with us. He'll take four liters from this morning's milking in payment." Mirian looked sideways from the griddle, a hot tortilla suspended in midair on her spatula and quietly but surely said, "Don Fernando, don't you think we should pay the pobrecita's way? We can spare eight liters." Nando knew she was right (and he also knew that, in the long run, he could never win a dispute that began with Mirian calling him Don Fernando), so he just sighed and nodded. Then Mirian thought out loud, "*Ojalá,* that my brother didn't come today instead of yesterday." Nando squinted with one eye, wrinkled his brow, and observed, "El Colombiano would have charged us two hundred lempiras and acted like he was showing us a great favor." Mirian knew he was right, so she just sighed and nodded.

She turned back to the little stove and lifted a small blue pot of steaming black beans from the banked cinders. She ladled the better portion of this into a large plastic bowl and snapped the lid on. She folded the four corners of the towel over the stacked tortillas and placed the bowl of frijoles on top. They could carry the food in the basket for the trip. All this Mirian did while deep in thought about other things. She thought about why Nando was right about her brother. She thought about the broken body laid out on Elizabet's bed. In her mother's heart, she was thinking, *So much hurt. We could have taken that little girl in. We could have fed another. I just didn't know.*

Nando had gathered up Arturo and Elizabet. Elizabet carried Arturo's mattress and sheet down to make a bed in the paila of the truck. Arturo followed with the plastic tarp that had many purposes. Today, it would be used to keep the rain first off the woman, and then off themselves, for the misty drizzle was descending again. On their return trip from the truck, they each carried a tambo or two of their neighbor's milk. They needed the room in the truck bed, and they clearly couldn't just leave it by the side of the road. They would store it in Mirian's kitchen until they returned with Alejandro for him to resume his morning route.

On their next trip, they carried Magdalena down to the truck on the anda that they had made and used to carry her to the house. It had been decided, again, without the need for discussion, that Elizabet and Arturo would ride in the back with the woman.

Nando would ride in the cabina with Alejandro. And, Mirian would stay at home with "her babies." They paused as they carried Magdalena past Doña Mirian, waiting on the porch outside the kitchen door. Mirian arranged Magdalena's hair again, as she would one of her own sleeping children. She kissed her forehead and stepped back, watching as her family carried Magdalena off the porch, across the yard, and down the lane toward the waiting truck. She stood there watching until they passed out of sight in the soft morning rain.

The ride to Hospital Loma de Luz from the back of a pick up was a familiar stretch of countryside played out backwards. Don Nando rode up front with Alejandro. They discussed with short observations in deep, early morning voices, the current events of the places and the people they passed. In the back, nothing was said. The wet countryside just rolled out a few yards at a time, diminishing into the distance with the road behind them. The Cordillera Santa Fe filled the lower sky over the tailgate, El Torre and Planes de Bambu loomed over the right rear fender, and then El Naranjito passed along the lee rail of the lechero's truck bed. Colonia Margarita, L'aldea de Allen, La Curva, Lucinda … the settlements passed by, wet, muddy and for the most part still. Few were out on this chilly, gray morning. Those who were on the road kept their heads down and their attention fixed on the next few muddy footsteps. In silence, Elizabet and Arturo watched all pass by from under the flapping dripping tarp.

About seven fifteen, they arrived at the gate of Hospital Loma de Luz. The gate was already open, but Alejandro knew he was not supposed to pass the gate until given permission by the *vigilante,* or "watchman," the guard at the gatehouse. At seven fifteen, the outpatient clinic was not yet open. It would be about a half an hour before the first gathering of patients would pass through the gate and climb the hill to the waiting room at the front of the hospital. These would be the patients with early clinic appointments and new patients with logistical considerations; an elderly man with a broken leg, who can neither sit nor stand, a single mother with a sick baby and five young children at home ... the patient, or their family, or a friend would petition the gate keeper/watchman. The watchman would radio the triage nurse, and these would be allowed up early.

But at seven fifteen, patients were just arriving and gathering out of the rain in the large open galera built just for that purpose. Workmen were arriving, as well as other young *mozos* looking for work while the change of shift of the guards was taking place. The oncoming watchman "de turno" at the gate this morning was Roberto Antonio Medina (de Jesus). Roberto's mother had always believed that the sun rose and set on her little Roberto Antonio. She always called him *Tonito.*

Tonito generally agreed with his mother's perspective on himself, but he did not like to be called Tonito. Basically everyone else along this coast of Colón couldn't understand what Tonito's mother

was on about, but they called him Tonito too. Both
Alejandro and Don Nando of course knew Tonito.
They could think back over a lifetime of playing and
working with him and agreed with the general consensus, but when he worked as the guard at the gate
of the hospital, they were both mature enough as
well as both Honduran enough to see him as a rep-
resentative of something greater than little Tonito.
In this case, they both showed due deference to
him in his role as gatekeeper at the hospital. They
both greeted him as Don Roberto (not Tonito) and
explained the situation in tandem. They both spoke
in the respectful third person instead of the *vos* they
had all used on the soccer field. And neither noticed
anything stilted or strange in this interchange. As
old Don Adolfo, Nando's father, often said, "*Aunque
el baile de la vida es un poco complejo, lo puede apren-
der.*" (Roughly, "although life's dance can be compli-
cated, you can still learn it.") Tonito listened to their
story with a grave air. He lifted the tarp with one
finger and peeked underneath with his lower lip and
chin pointing out unconsciously. Elisabet and Arturo
looked back wordlessly from under the tarp like two
half-soaked pups under the woodpile. Tonito could
see the unconscious young woman in a mixed school
uniform just behind them. She looked dead to him.

He stepped back into the shelter of the gatehouse and called on the radio to Molly Wilhoit, the
triage nurse on today's roster. In a half a minute she
responded. He had found her brushing her teeth and
getting ready for clinic.

"Doña *Moli,* this is Roberto at the gate. The lechero is here with a dead woman in the bed of his truck," Roberto reported.

"Well, what is she doing here if she's dead?"

"She is lying in the back of the truck."

"Well why is she *here* in the back of a truck?"

"I don't know. Maybe if they put her in the cabina then Nando would have to ride in the back, and he didn't want to get wet."

"Tonito, if she is dead, why did they bring her here instead of taking her to the Funeraria? "

"I don't know. Maybe this is closer."

She sighed. "Tonito, does the lechero think she is dead?"

"No, they don't know yet."

From this, the first radio exchange of the morning, you can see that Tonito was not the sharpest knife in the drawer, and while he was wrong not infrequently, he was never in doubt. Molly was the missionary nurse of the day. She was just coming on duty, and the day already had the makings of being another strange and unpredictable one. Molly had been personally convicted about her sometimes too-sharp tongue, and she had been trying hard to control it these past few months. After this last brilliant observation of Tonito's, Molly actually bit her tongue. She simultaneously thought of her resolution to hold her tongue and thought, *All sarcasm would be lost on Tonito anyway.* Then she felt a little badly for even thinking that. So she gave up on the Q and A and told Tonito to have the lechero bring the truck up to the emergency entrance at the back of the hospital and wait there. Tonito (or Don Roberto when on duty) actually raised his free hand in salute to the radio. He put on his most official face and stiffly waved the truck up from the road. Alejandro pulled up to the gate. Through the window, Tonito informed Alejandro that he was authorized to drive up to the door of the emergency entrance at the back of the hospital. He was to wait there. Taking one step back, Tonito stood up to attention and waved them up the hill with all pomp and circumstance.

Deference to precedence is one thing, but some guys just don't have any sense for where the boundaries are. As they drove up the hill, Alejandro rolled his eyes to Nando and asked, "You think he likes his job?" Nando lifted his eyebrows, thought a little, and offered, "Yes, like the monkey that ate the coconut, maybe a little too much."

# CHAPTER SEVEN

He sets on high those who are lowly, and those
who mourn are lifted to safety.

Job 5:11

The battered land cruiser pickup slowly followed
the drive past the front of the hospital, up the hill
to pass between and around various workshops and
warehouses, turning the corner and pulling up to the
emergency entrance at the back door. Both men knew
the way. They both had worked here. They both had
delivered materials here. They both had been treated
here for injuries or ailments at various times over
the years. Pulling in under the big metal *galera* and
now out of the drizzle, the old green Toyota began
to shed its fresh coat of rainwater, steam rising off
the rusting hood. Alejandro jumped out and set the
emergency brake (chocking the left rear wheel with
a wood block he kept behind the *cabina*).

Elisabet and Arturo stood up in the back of the

pickup, lifting the tarpaulin with them, spilling the water away from the motionless body between them. The back door of the hospital opened, and Duña, a serious-looking young woman of color, a *morena* as they say, in a nurse's uniform came walking directly down the sidewalk. Greetings were exchanged quickly but properly, and then responding to the questioning in her eyes, Don Nando briefly told *la enfermera* Duña how Arturo had found this young woman in an abandoned champa while searching for a wayward milk cow.

Though she looked very far gone, he thought she was alive, and so Alejandro the lechero had been kind enough to help them bring her in. Heads nodded all around as each in turn corroborated their part of the story.

Duña walked up to the pickup and peered inside. The young woman lying on the small mattress, dressed in a schoolgirl's uniform, looked rather dead. But it was Duña's duty to check her vital signs, and she was a little flummoxed as to how to get into the pickup while preserving the dignity of her role as a nurse. Alejandro, noticing her discomfiture, quickly lowered the tailgate and offered his hand for the nurse to step in. Duña, trying to keep her uniform clean while crouching beside the supine body on the damp mattress in the pickup bed, caught her breath. This woman wasn't dead. She had a pulse. Upon closer examination, she saw that the woman was breathing shallowly. And, there was no hiding the fact that this woman was very much *embarazada*, with child. Duña stood, and taking Alejandro's offered hand again, she hopped down onto the paving stones. Without making any commitments, she asked to be excused and walked up toward the hospital door while speaking into a hand-held two-meter radio. Molly had already called over and briefed Duña after her interchange with Tonito. Duña was calling Molly back to let her know that Tonito was mistaken. The lechero had it right. The woman, though she appeared gravely ill, was by no means dead yet. Duña entered through the hospital's double doors with the radio at her ear. Presently, she returned, backing through those doors pulling a gurney.

Elizebet and Arturo, who had been waiting on the sides of the pickup bed, positioned themselves at the head and feet of Magdalena as if they did this every day. They lifted her easily out of the paila of the Land Cruiser and onto the gurney that Duña had positioned alongside with the wheels locked. This was not the first patient that Duña had transferred out of a pickup truck bed. She strapped Magdalena on the narrow gurney and pulled the siderails up. Alejandro and Nando held the double doors open, and as she pulled the gurney between them, Duña instructed them that they could wait at the galera just outside the gate. "We will send word after the doctor sees her." Turning to the left and changing her position to push, Duña dismissed the men with a nod and a professional smile and shoved off in the direction of the emergency room.

Molly Wilhoit met Duña in the corridor outside

the emergency room. Molly had spoken to Duña by radio just as she was going out the door of the apartment. Hearing that Tonito's report of the demise of the woman in the back of the lechero's truck was somewhat premature, she came directly across the bridges and straight through the hospital. It was seven thirty-five now, and chapel devotions were just starting. Except for someone left to watch the in-patient wards, pretty much the entire staff on duty was there in the chapel courtyard now. So she imagined that Duña might need some help. Together, they brought Magdalena down to the emergency room, and together they began the initial assessment and resuscitation.

They checked her vital signs and began a flow sheet: pulse a thready 120, blood pressure 80/50, respiratory rate 34 and very shallow, but strangest and most worrisome of all, her temperature sublingually was 35.1 degrees Celsius (95,2 degrees Fahrenheit). Duña thought that the thermometer must be broken, so she tried a second one with the same results. "If the rain passes and the sun comes out, in an hour, that will be room temperature," Molly offered, mostly as a joke. As usual, Duña didn't recognize it as such and nodded her head gravely. It was also true after all.

Molly brought over a pulse oximeter and switched it on while Duña put the probe on Magdalena's cold blue-gray index finger. It registered her faint, too-fast pulse, but flashed out an $O_2$ saturation of 64 percent. Muttering something in English about nothing ever working, Molly took the probe off Magdalena's finger and put it on her own. The pulse immediately dropped to 72, and the saturation registered 99 percent. Molly and Duña looked at each other, then back to the monitor for a few heartbeats, then reconnected Magdalena to the pulse oximeter and rolled the $O_2$ concentrator over. They put her on mask $O_2$ from the concentrator at five liters per minute (as much as it would put out). Magdalena's $O_2$ saturation slowly climbed to 72 percent and stuck there.

Molly said to Duña, "I'll start an IV. You go check which doctor is coming on duty and ask him to come in here. I think it is Dr. Kevin. I saw him in chapel as I was passing." Each turned to their respective tasks at hand. Duña walked briskly into the chapel courtyard and then paused on the outskirts. She saw Dr. Kevin on the far side of the circle gathered in the middle of the courtyard. As unobtrusively as possible, she passed around behind the circle using the covered sidewalks at the edge of the courtyard. She came up quietly to stand behind him, hoping that he would just notice her. He didn't. He was lost in thought. The chapel meeting was at the point where prayer needs are shared. Dr. Kevin was listening to one of the cleaning staff sharing how troubled she was about the influence the high school teachers were having on her teenaged daughter. They made fun of Christians while filling her head with ideas *de socialismo.* Should she take her out of school? She just didn't know what to do. She had only finished third grade herself and sacrificed for her daughter to get an education. There were no other high schools in the *zona*. Should she trust the authorities that were so antagonistic to Christians? Dr. Kevin was puzzling over how that one should be sorted out when Duña tapped him on the shoulder.

Molly had quickly gathered all of the parts and pieces needed to start the IV. With the tourniquet on Magdalena's cold, thin arm, she looked carefully over the damaged skin and shook her head … the old scars from cigarette burns, half of a diez y ocho tattoo from the *mara*, "the gang," needle marks a couple of weeks old. This girl may have been found in a champa and was dressed in cheap schoolgirl clothes, but she was no schoolgirl from the campo. She clearly came from the city. Molly closed her eyes and tilted her head back and said under her breath, "Lord, help me." She had worked as an emergency room nurse at Charity Hospital in downtown New Orleans for two years before she came to believe she was meant to be a missionary. There, she had seen her share of what life on the streets would do to young girls. She had been away from that experience and on the field now for just over a year, so she still felt pretty good about her nursing skills. *At least better than my Spanish*, she thought. *I'm pretty good, but this is going to be a major league tough stick*, she thought. She said a quick prayer. And lo and behold, the prayer must have been answered. Molly found the brachiocephalic vein just above the antecubital fossa on Magdalena's right arm.

While searching for it, Molly mused that besides "not being from around here," based on the majority of needle marks being on her left arm, she was right handed. (Which was correct). Because there were still some possible sites remaining on her left arm and legs that this girl had not been using IV drugs for too long. (Also true.) Because there was a pretty good vein left on her right arm where the girl couldn't access it, but a "friend" could have. Molly guessed that this girl didn't have any such "friends" where she came from. Sadly, she was right again on that score.

Still, it was with a great sense of relief (and a little surprise) that Molly slid a twenty-gauge IV in on the first try. She was just taping the IV down and adjusting the rate when Duña returned with Dr. Kevin. Kevin Thompson had left the circle of the hospital staff's morning devotions at Duña's request for help with a patient in emergency. There had been no time for much explanation. So, as they entered the *sala de emergencias*, Duña gave a quick report. Molly finished the story with the current vital signs, physical findings, and O$_2$ saturation on the pulse oximeter. Duña, Molly, and Kevin stood around the gurney for a few minutes looking down on the used up, worn-out, and expectant little woman lying there as still as death.

Dr. Kevin, not given to much speech, said, "Got labs?"

"I just drew a purple top and a red top when I started the IV, but I was waiting to see what you would want to send them for," Molly said.

Kevin Thompson was young and quietly intense. Of West African extraction, born in Washington D.C., he had grown up in inner city Atlanta and had been trained n Boston. He was bright, driven, reserved... stiff even. He loved his wife and their two-year-old daughter fiercely, and when alone with them, he could loosen up and sometimes even laugh, but he was very serious about his work. He was very serious about his faith. In fact, he was very serious about almost everything.

Sometimes, when Molly interacted with Dr. Kevin in meetings or in clinic or when she watched him work so hard at other social interactions that should be easy, she thought, *He really needs to take lessons on lightening up.* But this morning she was glad he was the doctor of the day. He knew his stuff. And his training was in emergency medicine. And that is what this little mama needed just now.

Dr. Kevin said, "We'll need to check her electrolytes and CBC." He glanced again at the pulse oximeter. And pulling his stethoscope from the pocket of his clean and pressed white coat (which he wore every workday over scrubs, no matter how hot it was), he listened thoroughly to Magdalena's ragged, shallow breathing. "She'll need a chest X-ray. Is the developer still broken?"

Molly said, "I think so. I know that Suyapa was hand-dipping X-rays yesterday."

Dr. Kevin said to Duña in Spanish, "You have reported that the patient spent all night in the rain."

Duña replied, "Si, Doctor."

"Then we should believe that this temperature is probably correct. Let us begin her intravenous fluids of Dextrose 5 % in 0.45% saline solution at a rate of one hundred thirty-five ccs per hour. We should place a Foley catheter with a temperature probe, and we should wrap her in blankets and gradually warm her."

Duña replied, "Si, Doctor."

"And we will need to obtain anterior-posterior, and lateral radiograms of the chest."

Duña replied, "Si, Doctor."

Dr. Kevin's Spanish was much like Dr. Kevin's public persona: studied, careful, nearly always correct, and very stiff. It was an approach that had kept him alive in D.C.'s Anacostia, an approach that had gotten him out of the Kelvington Heights projects in Atlanta, and through medical school at Emory, an approach that helped him excel in his residency in Boston. Kevin knew that he came across kind of robotic. And he worked at seeming more relaxed and spontaneous. But it seemed the harder he worked at relaxing, the worse it got. Still, Kevin's wife, Janice, helped a lot. With Janice, he could relax. And, after two years at Loma de Luz, this life was beginning to take some of the starch out of his shorts.

Molly was thinking, without it really rising to consciousness, *Somebody has got to get us out of this "Si, Doctor" dialogue.* She continued (now in Spanish too), "So, where are we going to put her?" The ward was well staffed for the patient census that they had today. Duña was the charge nurse for the a.m. shift coming on, and she had two assistants, *Lisette* and *Jauncito*. But this one patient would require more time and care than ten ward patients. Duña's face was not hard to read. Magdalena did not look like a ward patient to her.

As nurse of the day, Molly's duties included filling in wherever needed and keeping the whole day moving ... more like nurse player/coach of the day.

"Have you seen the schedule for surgery yet today, Duña?" she asked.

"Yes, there are two patients for the repair of hernia. One is a child. There is a woman for hysterectomy. And there is a child with the cleft lip."

Molly nodded, thinking, *Good girl. She already thought to check the surgery schedule. She's a planner.* "Well, you never know what is going to come in, but that's not too bad. Only the hysterectomy and maybe the cleft lip will take much time in recovery."

Molly turned to Dr. Kevin. "I'm going to be in the recovery room this morning. With a little help, I can take care of her there this morning while I'm recovering patients. We've got Johanna and Celia in outpatient surgery, and we'll probably do the kids first. Probably no one but the hysterectomy will need much time, and I can call Celia in if I need help. So let's pull the partition in the back of the recovery room. I'll start thinking about coverage for the p.m. shift."

Kevin was nodding but said only, "Okay, let's keep her on the concentrator at five liters and warm her up slowly." All three gathered around Magdalena and moved her; lock, stock, and monitors down the hall near the operating suite, to the back of the room marked *sala de recuperación*. After getting her moved in, Kevin left to get a few things going, carrying Magdalena's blood with him to the lab. He promised to return in a few minutes to check on the patient and write admission orders.

Duña helped tidy up, pulled the partition, and took her leave. She promised to find Johanna or Celia and send them in. Molly checked Magdalena's vital signs and sat down at the desk to begin charting. Magdalena lay still and cold at the bottom of the deep, dark sea. She slept a dreamless sleep on the cusp of her long return to the surface, unaware of all the attention. Though she was utterly unaware of it, for the first time in Magdalena's brief and brutal life, she slept in a clean, dry, safe place, a place where people cared for her and even cared about her... for the first time in her life.

# CHAPTER EIGHT

Because I delivered the poor that cried, and the
fatherless, and him that had none to help him.

Job 29:12

Dr. Kevin dropped the blood off at the lab with orders
for the tests. Then he returned to the now empty chapel courtyard while the computer in his exam room
went through its laborious initiation protocol and
established connection with the router. He couldn't
stand what he thought of as "dead time." Kevin went
to the courtyard that morning for three reasons.
First, he needed to make a radio call, and he got better reception with his handheld two-meter radio out
there. Second, he liked the courtyard. It was quiet
and peaceful there, the kind of place that reminded
a person to pray. Then third, and for Kevin maybe
the most motivating, there, he could complete one of
the requirements in what his wife, Janice, called her
"LUKPRO," her Loosen Up Kevin Program. That

particular requirement was that three times each day
Kevin must stop and smell the roses. So each morning, he dutifully drank in the delightful fragrance rising from the dark pink floribunda roses that grew in
each corner of the courtyard. This morning he said
a prayer for the young woman they brought in from
the rain. Then he called his friend Ramon to ask him
to follow the young woman obstetrically.

Ramon Larios was a recent addition to the mission hospital's small but steadily increasing body of
national missionaries. He had grown up in San Pedro
Sula, had completed medical school at the Hospital Escuela in Tegucigalpa, and then went directly
to residency training in OB/GYN in Columbia. He
had never in his life before lived in the country, never
swam in anything but a swimming pool (except for
a few holidays at the beach in Tela). He had never
touched a cow and had never driven on a dirt road.
This might have been the same country as the one
that he was born and raised in, but it was a different
world. Still, when he heard from a friend of the possi-
bility to complete his year of obligatory social service
at Hospital Loma de Luz, he decided to exchange
his ticket with a former classmate. The placement
for social service in Honduras was decided by the
*Rifa,* "the raffle." Ramon, true to his "charmed life"
so far, had drawn Hospital Mario Catarino Rivas,
the big public health hospital in San Pedro Sula.
Besides being one of the most desired placements
in the Rifa, it was Ramon's hometown. His family
and his friends lived there. Yet, to the amazement of

friends and family, and somewhat to his own bewilderment, he traded in his ticket for the city that he knew for the mud and the sweat and the manure of the campiño, the "rural outback" (which was completely foreign to him). He thought it was time to put feet to his faith, caring for the poor of his own country. He had finished his *servicio* the previous year and again surprised most everyone by asking to stay on as a missionary there. His application was accepted.

So Dr. Kevin Thompson, who grew up about as poor and "underprivileged" as it gets in one of the richest countries in the world, called on the two-meter radio to his friend Dr. Ramon Larios, who grew up about as well-off and privileged as it gets in one of the poorest countries in the world. The ties that bound them were more important than their disparate backgrounds.

Dr. Kevin called, "HR3 HDL, HR3 HDL, KC6IDT here. Dr. Larios, Dr. Larios, Do you copy?"

During the pause while waiting for a response, Kevin thought, *HDL, I wonder every time I call Ramon if he thinks of high density lipoproteins when he hears HDL? I wonder how they organize the words in Spanish.*

Dr. Ramon replied, "Good morning, *hermano* Kevin. How are you?"

"Fine, I'm fine."

"How is Janice this morning?

"She's much better too. Thank you."

"And little Christina? How is her cough?"

"She's much better. Thank you."

"Well, my friend, what can I do for you?"

"Uhhmmm. Perhaps we should get off the open channel."

"Oh, yes. I always forget."

"Yes, then, QSY to one four six five hundred?"

"Yes, QSY."

In a community that communicates by two-meter radio, a specific frequency that all monitor will be designated as the "open channel," or "party line." The open frequency, for instance, in this case, was 146.550 Mhz. One will then QSY, or change frequencies, to a different frequency nearby to carry on a conversation. On the designated fifty to seventy-five people at any given time, Dr. Kevin laid out for Dr. Ramon what he knew so far about Magdalena.

After Dr. Keven explained the situation, Dr. Ramon asked, "Do we yet know the fetal heart rate?"

"I'm sorry. You were breaking up. Could you repeat your last? Over."

"Yes, I think my battery needs charging."

"Did not copy all after 'I think.' Sounds like your battery is low."

Yes, my friend. I'll keep my transmissions short." (*Transmitting uses much more amperage than receiving.*)

Dr. Kevin strained to hear. "Did not hear all after *friend.* Maybe you should keep your answers short."

Dr. Ramon, spacing his words slowly, said, "Yes. Fetal Heart Rate? Over."

Kevin, whose battery was fine and could transmit any length of message, replied, "It was really pretty hard to find. The mother's blood pressure was barely appreciable … maybe sixty systolic. We hadn't set up the Doppler yet. But I listened with the fetal stethoscope, and I think I caught it briefly. I didn't catch it long enough to get an accurate rate."

"Water broken? Discharge?"

"Don't know yet. Haven't completed the exam. Still stabilizing her."

"Don't worry. I'll come see her before clinic and do the ultrasound."

"Sorry, missed all after 'don't worry.'"

"I'll … see … her."

"Copy that. Copy that. Thank you, Ramon. Will check with you later. So, KC6 IDT, QSY to one four six point four hundred and standing by."

Kevin looked into the cracked but still functional LCD of his handheld radio. He watched as he spun frequencies from his set channel number three, 146.500, to his set channel number two, 146.400, the frequency for the physician on call. Then he pressed function and six to lock it. The handheld bumped off frequency too easily, so Kevin always locked it methodically on the desired frequency before he replaced it on his belt between the last and the second to the last loop. Yes, he's a little obsessive compulsive, but that's not necessarily such a bad thing in a physician.

While unconsciously resetting his radio, Kevin was subconsciously working out some problem with the way he had left the orders regarding the young woman in the ICU. There was some disorder in his orders. Kevin couldn't quite bring to mind yet what it was, but the uneasy feeling was already driving his feet toward the south hall exit of the chapel courtyard, on the most direct route back to the recovery room/makeshift ICU. Yet, just as his left foot reached the outer sidewalk, his subconscious brain said, "Stop!" His mouth said, "Whoops." He turned an about-face and retraced ten steps to the blushing rosebush, which shyly waited in the southwest corner of the courtyard. Stiffly, formally, Kevin bent at the waist and dutifully inhaled the delightful fragrance. "There," he said, straightening thoughtfully. "That makes two. Once more this afternoon will make three for Janice. Still," he mused, "that was rather nice. Now where was I? Oh yeah, chest X-ray."

Opening the door into the sala de recuperacion (*cum* temporary ICU), Dr. Kevin found Molly seated on a stool at an elevated patient tray table, charting.

"Listen, I was thinking, when I told Duña we'll need a chest X-ray on this lady, I wasn't very clear. Obviously, she can't stand for an X-ray in the radiology suite. We'll just have to get a portable."

"Already got it. Celia came in and helped me with the c-arm before the first case started. It's being developed now. Based on your orders to Duña, I tried tying her up to the chest bucky and hanging her there, but the Kerlex wouldn't hold. But hey, you're the doctor."

Kevin blushed under his dark skin until his ears burned. "Yes … umm … well … good job. I should have been clearer. I'll go start clinic. I'll come back to write orders when the lab is done." Dr. Kevin backed out of the room so abruptly and shut the door so quickly you might have thought he had walked into the women's bathroom by mistake. As the door clicked shut, Molly smacked herself on the forehead with the heel of her hand; then she put her head in her hands with her elbows on the tray table and her eyes screwed shut. "Oh Lord, when will I ever change? That wasn't funny. It was just ugly. Sheesh! Why can't I ever keep my sarcastic mouth shut?"

*Here I was patting myself on the back for not going off on Tonito, and an hour later I bludgeon Dr. Kevin like that over nothing. Then he takes it with more grace than I've ever shown. There must be a thousand pagans within five miles that act more Christian than me. Here I wanted to be this great missionary, but I'm just the same ... just a failure.* Praying, soul searching, pity party, taking an inventory, or e.), all the above, Molly had little time to continue in this vein. The first operation of the day would be finished shortly. You might remember that Molly was covering the recovery room, as well as acting as ICU nurse for Magdalena. The first case was a pediatric hernia and was done quickly and without difficulty under IV sedation and regional anesthesia. The little boy, Darwin Robles, should have been a pretty simple recovery, but for a local kid he had been uncharacteristically uncooperative.

Campesinos tend to be stoic, cooperative, and appreciative patients., even the children. But Darwin whined when he came in, pitched a little fit about getting into the hospital gown, fought the IV placement in pre-op, and just generally couldn't be controlled, something which his mama didn't even seem to attempt to do. He had all of the earmarkings of *el niño concentido*, "the concented child." In English, you would say "spoiled" or "out of control." Spanish is much less direct and confrontational, so in this case, less pejorative. But the behavior is the same. To get that behavior to a more manageable state, Sandi, the anesthetist, had decided to give him a three mg/kg IM dose of Ketamine in the holding area before surgery. Within a few minutes, Darwin had the thousand-yard stare and paid no attention when Sandi started the IV. Very little more was needed to augment the sedation during the case. But, as they brought him to recovery, Darwin was awakening from one of those strange Ketamine dreams. Celia helped Molly keep the little boy from climbing over the rail of the gurney and from pulling out his IV. After his first set of vital signs were recorded, Celia went off to get his mother to help watch him as he slowly returned to this plain, old boring world from the apparently very bizarre and interesting planet Ketamine. Celia then went off to help with the next case, another child, this one with a cleft lip. That one, of course, would be a general anesthetic.

His mama's help notwithstanding, Molly had her hands full with Darwin for the next half hour. It was just at the end of that hectic half hour that Dr. Ramon Larios stepped in the door of the recovery/intensive care room. Molly looked up from checking Magdalena's blood pressure manually (to cross check the Dynamap's readings). She caught Darwin's left hand in midair for the twentieth time as it headed for the IV in his right hand. For the eighteenth time, she handed the hand to Darwin's mama and said, "Could you hold this please ?"

For the fifth time in fifteen minutes, Molly tucked behind her ear a stray shock of hair that had escaped from ponytail and hat. She straightened, thinking, *Oh brother, I bet I'm a sight ... ran over here right out of the shower, no makeup, goofy hat. All I need is to be holding a bedpan to top off my ensemble.*

Dr. Larios often flustered Molly. She liked being around him. It seemed everyone did. He was kind and gracious and always seemed sort of amused in a cultured sort of way. That seemed to be part of the problem for Molly. By comparison, without meaning to do so, and without noticing it, Ramon always made Molly feel sort of reckless and unsophisticated and not put together. Ramon's presence made her feel ... well ... the opposite of Ramon.

"Good morning, Dr. Larios,"

"Good morning, good morning, Miss Molly. How did you awaken?"

"Well, I guess I awoke okay, but it has gone all downhill from there."

"Oh, and downhill is bad?"

"Yes, I suppose that's an expression that would be hard to anticipate."

"Most assuredly. I am often impressed by what I do not know about the English language. I was always considered good at it in school you know.

But, working with you, my North American friends, I find that, as you say, I don't know the half of it."

"Uhh … yeah."

"So, how is our patient?"

"You mean the Rainwoman? Well, she doesn't talk much. But, I think she's warming up to us. *Watch your funny mouth girl,*" thought Molly to herself. "Her core temp is up to thirty-six point one Celsius [ninety-seven degrees Fahrenheit]."

"Yes, well, I have the ultrasound machine here in the hall. Would now be a good time to have a look at the baby?"

"Sure, I guess now would be pretty good. I was just finishing up with a round of everybody's vital signs. I won't be due for another patient for twenty or thirty minutes. And I think my main man Darwin here is beginning to chill."

Ramon really did not have a clue for how to respond to that, so he just brought the portable ultrasound machine into the room and maneuvered it around and between gurneys and monitoring equipment. As he went through the initial start-up algorithm with the ultrasound, Ramon asked Molly what she knew about the patient. Molly told him what she knew … which wasn't very much. "So, the way I see it, a mystery woman gets used up and thrown away in the big city. Somehow, for who knows what reason, she winds up out here at the end of the road in the rainy season. She spends last night (or who knows how long) out in this weather and comes in hypothermic, 'on death's door,' and she can't even tell us her name.

Moving the ultrasound probe around expertly on Magdalena's little belly, Ramon's eyes stayed on the monitor. But, turning his chin a bit over his shoulder toward Molly, he continued to carry on a pleasant conversation. "So, you call her the Rainwoman, like the film with Dustin Hoffman and Tom Cruise, because she can't tell you her name?"

The question caught Molly off guard. Still stinging from having hurt Kevin Thompson's feelings with her sharp tongue, the question elicited a flustered tempest of words all a jumble that Ramon found hard to follow. "What? No, I never even saw that old movie. And, I'm not cruel and sarcastic to helpless, unconscious people…well maybe Tonito sometimes. I'm just sarcastic to my friends. And how do you know so much about American movies? I just called her the Rainwoman because…well, we don't know her name, and just like a little bird that I found all wet after a storm when I was a little girl that I called the rainbird, they brought her in out of the rain all helpless so…I just called her the Rainwoman. I didn't mean anything by it."

Mercifully, the opening of the door saved Ramon from trying to follow that stream of consciousness to its source. It was Dr. Kevin. He stuck his head in the door first, sort of tentatively, as you would if you thought someone inside might throw a shoe at you as soon as you stepped inside. With his body still outside and his neck craning around the door, he said, "Hello, Ramon." And, nodding in her direction, he said "Molly. How's she doing?"

"Well, she's warming up." Core temperature's a whopping thirty-six point three degrees Celsius now. But I can't get her $O_2$ saturation above eighty-six on five liters by the concentrator.

Kevin came on in through the door as he continued, "Yes, I saw her chest X-ray. She's got bilateral patchy infiltrates. I have an idea that after she gets hydrated and warmed up, we'll see a full-blown bilateral pneumonia…maybe ARDS. I'm thinking that we may have to put her on the ventilator. How does the baby look, Ramon?"

"Well my friend, I can definitely say that there is another person in the room. He looks a little sleepy, but he's not too shy. As best I can tell by this portable, another son of the race and lineage of Adam is soon to be born. I have yet to complete the measurements, but I would say that our little Rainwoman is in the last month of her pregnancy."

Kevin nodded again and cleared his throat as he did when he was uncomfortable, and then said, "There is one more thing that should be kept in mind by every person caring for her. I just came from the lab. We'll have to send it off to Tegucigalpa for confirmation with the western blot, but on the chromatography screening tests, this woman is strongly HIV positive."

# CHAPTER NINE

---

I waste away: I will not live forever. Leave me
alone, for my days are but a breath.

Job 7:16

Except for the humming rasp of the oxygen concentrator and the metronomic piping of the cardiac monitor, silence had the floor in the room for
a moment. Then Ramon broke the silence with a
long, audible sigh, followed by "Dios Mio. *Como si
esto fuera poco,*" a saying sort of like "as if this weren't
enough."

Kevin seconded, "yeah."

Ramon continued, now in English, "We must
treat her, of course, with the mixed agent protocol if
we can, to protect the baby at least. Do you know if
we have Combivir in stock?"

Kevin answered, "I know we have Zidovudine and
Nelfinavir, but I'm not sure that they're 'in-dates'. I
do know that we only have them in tablets. We don't

have any IV anti-virals. Just didn't think we'd be treating a comatose HIV positive woman late in pregnancy. I'll see if we can get some shipped in, but first things first. I also checked on her white count, and it is twenty-eight hundred … not good in the face of the bilateral pneumonia. I think we can get a CD4 count in La Ceiba, and we can stage her pretty well otherwise. But, if we can't get on top of her pneumonia, well … this woman needs a lot of prayer."

With his excellent sense of timing, Ramon suggested, "Well then, my friends, why don't we start now?" And so they did. For, Loma de Luz, despite its shortcomings in supplies and sophisticated equipment, is a Christian mission hospital. And Ramon, Kevin, and Molly, despite their own shortcomings, are Christian missionaries. If there is one thing that distinguishes the missionary from other tribes of zealots, it is not that they are exceptionally smart or good looking, unusually holy, or easy to get along with. Not infrequently, they are none of the above. No, instead, it is just this: for whatever the reason, like the old Nike saying, they are the tribe most likely to "just do it." They come to believe that God says go, and they're gone. They become convinced that God wants them to carry the word to the Hibi Tree People, and they start practicing tree-climbing.

And when they say, "We should pray about that," they're dropping their heads and closing their eyes. So Kevin, Ramon, and Molly prayed then and there. They even believed that God was listening. They believed, among other things, that He was the "present observer." They believed that He might do something about it. They even believed that it might make a difference if they asked. As it turns out, He was, and He did, and it mattered.

There was nothing much that you could see or hear that took place. After they each took a turn to thank God for being present, listening, and able, they simply asked that He would help and heal little Magdalena (though they didn't yet know her name). Each one opened their eyes about the same time. The monitor still called out the same cadence. The $O_2$ concentrator still hoarsely hummed the same tune. Molly walked over and put her hand on Magdalena's cheek, which still felt like death, not yet warmed over.

But from that instant, the instant that Molly touched her cheek, Magdalena's body began to mount an effective immune response. On the cusp of the twenty-first century, when this story takes place, science had only begun to learn the alphabet of the immune response, the body's elegant and incredibly complex yet entire and integrated symphonic response to infection and injury. Oh, we knew enough to fill a few textbooks with hazy outlines about the cascade of events on the molecular level that drives the recognition of foreign proteins then captures and destroys them while remembering what they were vulnerable to, and creating a slumbering machinery better prepared for another similar assault. But, our understanding then was nothing more than an unsure recognition of a melody. Even now, though enough knowledge of its inner workings have been painstakingly puzzled out in the intervening years to fill digital vaults with a daunting mass of raw data ... a truly encompassing score for this symphony is still many years in the future. The most knowledgeable few of our race who understand the sketchiest outline of this grand symphony know that they don't know the half of it. They recognize the melody lines and realize that there is much more to it. And when they are really honest about it, they suspect that someone wrote the score. The irreducible minimum of the hundreds of thousands of inter-related molecular and sub-molecular events necessary to mount an effective immune response simply statistically could not have happened by chance.

Neither did the initiation of Magdalena's recovery. Nor, to be honest, did it begin by Magdalena rising from the dead and making her bed. It was a little more subtle than that. For the next six hours, she looked pretty much the same. That is, metabolically speaking, she continued pretty much on par with a starfish. Except of course, that she did warm up.

As she moved up the phylogenetic scale, she did begin to cough, and she did begin to moan, but you couldn't say that she was conscious. Her $O_2$ saturation on the pulse oximeter hovered between 79 and 81 percent on five liters per minute from the oxygen concentrator. Her blood pressure came up a little to roughly 86 over 50. But, her pulse stayed about 120.

At noon, Celia and Marta knocked tentatively on the recovery room/ICU door. When Molly opened the door, they presented her with a lunch that they had put together from parts of their own. They knew that Molly had come over to the hospital right out of the shower and without a lunch in hand. It was—surprise!—rice and beans and a tortilla. Of course, their lunch every day consisted of rice and beans and a tortilla, so I guess that shouldn't have been too astonishing. Molly was touched by their humble and unassuming generosity. For both Celia and Marta (who was nursing her second baby and always hungry), it cost the prospect of finishing the largest meal of the day still a little hungry. But this kind of quiet unassuming sharing was as natural to them as it would have been unnatural for them to leave Molly to miss a meal or, worse yet, to spend lunchtime all alone by herself, no matter what she had to eat. So they pulled in a couple of chairs and an empty Mayo tray table on wheels and shared the noon meal together in the front of the recovery room.

About three thirty p.m., Duña, Mel Flores, and Ana Lynn Dalton came over. Clinic was winding down. In the operating room, they were closing on the hysterectomy, the last elective operation of the day. Duña was, you might remember, the off-going charge nurse from the a.m. shift. Mel was coming on as the p.m. charge nurse. Ana Lynn had been doing some administrative work in the library and knew that she was coming on as the on call R.N. for that night. Mel was an *infermera auxiliar,* essentially, a vocational nurse, and a good and generally experienced one. But, he had no critical care training or experience and knew it … neither did Ana Lynn.

After nursing school, Ana Lyn Dalton had spent two years working on a medical/surgery ward at a community hospital, then ten years running a urologist's outpatient clinic. After three years on the field at Loma de Luz, she had learned to be a pretty good triage nurse and ward nurse, and she was naturally a good administrator. But she too was intimidated by the critical care patient. Both Mel and Ana Lynn had heard about Magdalena, and they both knew that what she needed in the way of nursing care was out of their depth in critical care. They had all come over to talk with Molly to try to figure out how they could cover the nursing care for the little Rainwoman.

Standing in a tight clutch inside the recovery room, but near the door, they first asked how she was doing. "She seems to be recovering from the hypothermia and dehydration, but as she does, her pneumonia seems to blossom. Core temperature is thirty-seven point two degrees Celsius [ninety-nine degrees Fahrenheit] her pulse is one-ten, and blood pressure one hundred over seventy, but her $O_2$ saturation on five liters is still seventy-nine. She's gotten pretty wet on her lung sounds in the past hour. I've turned her and done chest P.T. Have to suction her about every ten minutes, but when I do, she drops her saturation into the sixties. I've talked with Dr. Kevin about intubating her and putting her on the ventilator. But he thinks that it's not working reliably, something about an o-ring seal. Now that she's warmed up, her eye signs aren't so weird, and she now responds to pain. She withdrew her arm when I pushed the Imipenem, and she gags when I suction her ... but she still won't cough spontaneously ... and, bottom line is ... she's gotta cough."

Molly's rapid-fire monologue had come out like an ICU report at change of shift. From the uneasy silence that followed, and the glances from side to side by the other nurses, it was clear that several points needed clarification. So the next fifteen minutes were spent in slowly working through Magdalena's condition in Spanish, avoiding or explaining some of the jargon. After all, Duña understood some but spoke no English. Mel spoke some island English but had understood maybe half of the report, and Ana Lynn had a few questions about "saturation dropping into the sixties" and "pushing the Imipenem."

After all was explained, discussed, and considered regarding where they stood with Magdalena, there followed another half a minute of uneasy silence while each considered what could be done for nursing coverage. Then blowing out a heavy breath, Ana Lynn said, "Gracious be!"

Mel whistled a falling tone.

Duña just said, "Si!"

After another few thoughtful seconds, Ana Lynn thought out loud, "Well, maybe she should be transferred to *Atlantida*."

Molly, clearly having already thought that option out, like a reflex arc, simply stated, "She'd never make it." Whether she meant the trip to get there, or the stay in Atlantida, or either one, there was no need to discuss that point. The trip was at least an hour and a half over rough roads in the best of times, but now, ruined by the rainy season and worsened by the last forty-eight hours of constant rain, the *plancha* on the approach to the *Lis Lis* bridge was said to be under three feet of water. The approach to the bridge itself had been undercut to less than a risky single lane, and the ford at the *Quebrada Limeras* was running bank to bank, four feet high and rising. Even if they could arrange a multi-car transfer involving cars on each side of two little rivers with dugout canoes in the crossing, the trip would take at least three hours. Even if she survived to the gate of the hospital Atlantida, the sprawling, dilapidated, perennially overwhelmed, and understaffed and woefully undersupplied public health hospital in La Ceiba, they would almost assuredly spend hours trying to get her through admissions and evaluated in the emergency room, only to find that there were no more critical care beds, then have her shipped on to *Hospital Caterino Rivas* in San Pedro Sula, dying somewhere en route ... a route that the more jaded ambulance drivers called the *"funerale expreco,"* "rapid delivery to your funeral."

Again, in short, "She'd never make it."

They all considered their short list of options while looking at the floor. After a few more short seconds, Mel thought out loud for them all, "Like we say, '*entre la espada y la pared.*'" (Literally, "between the sword and the wall.")

Molly liked learning Spanish aphorisms and

responded, "Oh, I get it, like we say, 'Between a rock and a hard place.'"

Duña just folded her arms and said, more like a command than a suggestion, "*Ya oremos!*" (Let's pray.) Then, without waiting for confirmation, she dropped her arms to her sides and clenched both fists. She rocked back and forth between the balls of her feet and her heels in a posture all her own. With eyes tightly shut, she launched off into four minutes of very loud, fluid, and impassioned prayer. After four minutes and fifteen seconds of pouring out her heart and having run to the end of her petition, Duña just shut it off with an abrupt, "Amen." Her "amen" was seconded and passed by consensus. Then, not two seconds after the last supporting "amen" was aired, Magdalena, from the back of the room and the depths of that dark well of souls, first coughed, then moaned, then coughed again and again until she struggled to inhale.

What happened next was a stunned silence. Funny how we call out to God so fervently, but we are shocked and scared or doubtful when He answers. Duña closed her mouth first, and then said in wonder, "*Gloria a Dios!*" Mel, who was a half-second behind her on the uptake, but was about to reflexively say something more profane, thought better of it, and just said, "*Asi es*" (That's it).

Molly had been thinking about (and secretly hoping that someone would rescue her from) volunteering for more work. She had formulated a plan, but she was waiting for a sign all the same. With this nudge, this evidence that Magdalena was going to try to live, she laid out her plan. "Okay, look. Adrianna is coming on as charge nurse in the morning right?" She looked to Duña, who nodded affirmation. "Well, she worked the ICU at *D'Ántoni* the last eight months before she came out here. Duña, if you can cover for her as charge tomorrow, she can take care of our little Rainwoman. Duña again nodded her assent. Ana Lynn, if you can stay with her for a few hours, I'll go take a nap and come back here at six thirty, and then I can stay with her tonight. Dr. Kevin is still here in clinic in case you have questions, and I'll check you out on the monitors and meds before I go.

Ana Lynn looked a little uneasy but hardly paused at all before saying, "Well sure, hon." So that is what they did.

At six thirty in the evening, Molly got a ride back over to the hospital with Jim Coble. Jim was staying at staff housing for a couple of months, helping out with hospital maintenance. He was heading back over to the hospital bodega/workshop side after supper, driving the communal gold Ford pickup. He was planning to work in the shop on some shelves he was building and e-mail his wife on the office PC via the hospital's satellite Internet connection. He dropped Molly off at the front door of the hospital, her arms loaded with a sack lunch, a coffee pot, and a well-worn copy of Chesterton's *Father Browning Mysteries*.

She stood there in the drive for a moment, looking out to sea. The *Cayos Cochinos* stood out, an indigo armada under a slate gray mantle of clouds. The sky between storm clouds and these islands glowed all of the fire colors from the banked embers of the sun just recently gone over the edge of the world. She stood there in the gravel road, her hair still wet from the evening shower, her arms full of the night's provisions, unaware of all but the painfully beautiful sky and sea. Without actually knowing it, she softly sang *en soto voce* a couple of lines from an old hymn, "Oh Lord my God, when I in awesome wonder, consider all the worlds thy hands have made." Then it began to drizzle, and with a peaceful and private look still on her face, Molly turned and walked into the hospital.

Buildings share a lot in common with people. They have personalities and quirks, flaws and rhythms, and daily cycles. A hospital in the evening, to those accustomed to them, is a quietly reassuring place.

The work-a-day bustle and hustle and energy of the a.m. shift had passed. The still solemnity and solidity of the night shift was yet to come. Families were visiting. Voices were subdued but not hushed. Meals were being finished, and the patients were beginning to settle in for the night. Molly walked through the wards and paused at the nursing station, talking briefly with Mel and the nursing techs, and then turned to cross through the chapel courtyard. Patients and family members sitting on benches in the courtyard exchanged smiles and pleasant *saludos* as Molly passed. Turning, she continued past the emergency room and back to the recovery/ICU.

She found Ana Lynn busy suctioning Magdalena. She turned and looked up when Molly entered, her hair uncustomarily frazzled, with a mixture of relief and accomplishment on her face. Ana Lynn was a heavyset, motherly woman from outside of Waycross, Georgia. She called everyone "hon." From a tough start in the middle of the pack of thirteen sharecropper's kids, through an abusive marriage at seventeen, through raising three small children alone on a waitress's salary, Ana Lynn had worked her way through life. She had worked her way through an associate's degree in business college (the first in her family to get past high school). She had worked her way through nursing school. And she kept being pleased and surprised in life by accomplishing things that she'd always been told were far beyond her. All of her children had college degrees now, and here she was, a missionary nurse taking care of a critical care patient all alone. Just before Molly's knock on the door, she had wiped the sweat off her forehead and thought to herself, *It's a world of wonder ... if only my granny could see me now ... I wonder if she can.*

Presently, Ana Lynn reviewed with Molly all that she had done and observed and how the little Rain-woman was responding. After telling her tale in an orderly and sensible fashion, she shifted from nurse to mother. Peering into Molly's face and touching her arm, she asked, "You gonna be all right, hon?"

Molly nodded and answered, "Sure."

Ana Lynn smiled and said, "Well all right then." Then she slipped out into the evening, closing the door behind her.

# CHAPTER TEN

What is man that you magnify him, and that you
are concerned about him?

Job 7:17

Molly, of course, did fine. She worked hard on Magdalena but also read a little, walked through the still
dark hospital a few times, and finished most of a pot
of coffee. Though Magdalena continued in critical
condition and her numbers were pretty marginal,
that night she began the long road of recovery. Too
weak to manage much for herself, she required careful but aggressive support with fluid and diuretic balance, broad spectrum antibiotics, cardiac meds, and
constant respiratory care.

Making what decisions she could on her own,
Molly, who was pretty confident and competent in
critical care, still called Dr. Kevin three times that
night. Yet, by the first shift of the air from indigo
to violet over the Cordillera de San Antonio to the

east, Magdalena was a little more stable, her lungs a little more clear, and her heart a little stronger. As the light from the window strengthened, Magdalena opened her eyes. She blinked at first, unseeing, her sight still internal, her mind still adrift in the wordless dreams of her dark sleep. But without any conscious desire to come back, her body was able, and the morning light anchored her thoughts. From that anchored point Magdalena's mind began to reorder itself, to make sense of the images the light brought to her eyes. The realization settled that she was back in this world, the world of misery. Other than weak and sick, she felt only a dull disappointment. She realized that she would have to re-enter *la lucha*, the struggle to survive, and she remembered her despair. Then her hands came to rest on her belly and the new life within. She remembered the reason why she had to come back. She groaned and coughed and closed her eyes. Then with an effort she opened them again, taking in the room, the machinery, and then she focused on Molly.

They studied each other. After a moment Molly said, *"Buenos Días. ¿Como se siente?"* (Good morning. How do you feel?) Magdalena just nodded then closed her eyes and slipped back into the world of dreams on the other side of the tapestry between worlds.

In this way, one foot in one world and one foot in the next, Magdalena came and went for several days. Yet each day, by God's grace, she grew a little stronger. And each time she returned to this world, she stayed a little longer. Still not speaking, she watched everything: the lights, the monitors, the ritual recording of vital signs, and Is and Os, those who brought and who cleared away the meals, which she ate in watchful silence. But more than anything, she watched those who cared for her.

On the morning of the fifth day since Don Nando and Alfredo the lechero had brought Magdalena to Hospital Loma de Luz, Molly was again coming on duty to care for her. It had become pretty clear that she was recovering. Indeed, Molly was planning to ask Dr. Kevin when he came in for morning rounds about transferring Magdelena out of the makeshift ICU and over to a modified step-down unit on the inpatient wards. She had recovered now to the point that she could receive pretty much the same care that she was receiving in the one-on-one ICU. The manpower/womanpower cost of one-on-one nursing care was really starting to put a strain on the staff.

Magdalena was awake this morning. And, as she was whenever she was awake, she was watching. Molly came in and met Magdalena's gaze. *"Buenos Diás."* Magdalena nodded but said nothing. She had not spoken a word since her painful and disappointed return into this world three mornings earlier. Molly set down her *mochila* (her knapsack) and her coffee cup. She still held onto the clipboard that Adriana had turned over to her. In the checkout in the hallway outside, Adriana had gone over all that had transpired with Magdalena on the nightshift, all neatly recorded on the graphic record and nurse's notes on the clipboard. Then she had turned that over to Molly like the passing of a relay baton. Molly glanced over the record again and set it down on the side table. She checked Magdalena's blood pressure, pulse, and temperature, her oxygen saturation, gathered the lab work that had just come in, and set them all down in their places on the chart. Then she pushed the clipboard aside and sipped from her cooling cup of coffee.

Looking directly in Magdalena's face (who was looking back at her), she asked, "*¿Pues? ¿Cómo le llaman?*" (So what do they call you?) Magdalena's face barely moved a muscle, but Molly thought she saw pain in her eyes. She tried a slightly different track and said, "*¿Entonces? Cómo te llamas?* (Then, what do you call yourself?)

Magdalena looked directly back but said nothing for a long minute, long enough that Molly began to wonder if she understood; if she could even speak. As she raised her eyebrows, frowned, and began to look away, Molly heard a hoarse whisper, "Magdalena."

Molly turned back and asked "*¿Perdón? ¿Que dijo?*" (What did you say?)

Magdalena, her expression never changing, whispered again slowly, "Magdalena."

"Magdalena, es con mucho gusto. Me llamo Moli." (Pleased to meet you, Magdalena. I'm Molly). "*¿Y su apellido?*" (And your last name?) Magdalena made a small shake of her head and looked away. This was all that Molly would hear on the subject today. In fact, that was all that Magdalena would allow on any subject for many more days.

It wasn't that Magdalena was pouting or that she was unappreciative of the care and the hard work that was being lavished on her. She was just struggling with the crushing depression commonly seen in those recuperating from near-death experiences. She was struggling just to eat, to watch, and to sleep. Taciturn by nature, in such a deep depression, she just couldn't bring herself to talk. But she did get better. Over the next four days, she moved from the ICU to the step-down unit, to the regular ward. So, recently on IV fluids only, she went from clear liquids to full liquids, to a regular diet; from the bed, to walking down the hall. She even began to receive visitors … well, one visitor.

On a Friday, nine days after her arrival at Loma de Luz, and her first full day on the regular ward, at nine o'clock in the morning, Doña Mirian came through the door of the women's ward and walked up to Magdalena's bedside. In a place where cars were rare, and phones rarer still, how did a woman with neither phone nor car living miles away from the hospital learn that a friendless, nameless, sick woman was being moved to the regular ward and could therefore receive visitors? That kind of question could rarely be answered out here. But somehow news traveled fast down those dirt roads.

Mirian might have felt unsure or out of place as she stood there at Magdalena's bedside. But she walked in with the dignity and imperturbable poise of a strong woman who has known small successes and great losses … and survived them all. She had given birth to seven children and raised them all through God's provision and grace. One was crippled, one was simple, one had died, and another was alone and far from home. This young woman in the bed wasn't much older than her Adolfo would have been. She was no weaker than Rosalia had been with the crippling fever and no more able to care for herself than Mona.

Now Mirian pulled a chair up near Magdalena's bedside, sat down, leaned forward and said, "Good morning, Magdalena. It makes me glad to see that you are doing better. I am Mirian Ortiz Garcia. Do you remember me?" Magdalena simply stared back and said nothing. "I knew your grandmother Doña Ondina quite well. Your family's farm is next to ours. I knew you when you were a little girl. Still, Magdalena's face did not change.

But, she opened her mouth and asked in a voice rusty and raspy from long disuse; "¿A donde fueron?" (Where did they go?)

Now Mirian waited a moment before answering, "Your Abuelita became ill and died here in this hospital two years ago. I understand that she had a cancer." Again, a long silence settled. Magdalena's face still did not move, but her eyes widened and blurred with unshed tears. "I don't think she suffered much," Mirian presently added, in hopes that it might later be a comfort to the girl. "She died at peace with the Lord. But I know she worried about you."

Now a tear spilled over and rolled down into Magdalena's hair. Still she did not move. In a moment, Mirian continued gently but steadily. "The children went here and there. I believe two of your cousins are staying in Rio Coco and one in Lucinda. The rest I understand are in La Ceiba or San Pedro." Mirian then sat quiet and patient and after some time finished with, "I'm sorry."

Magdalena lay there without a sound, her face still motionless, her eyes staring off beyond Mirian, tears silently flowing down into her hair. Mirian stayed. After a few more long, pregnant moments passed, Magdalena sniffed, coughed, and rolled to her side. With her back to Mirian and her face turned toward the wall, she shuddered; then her shoulders began to heave in silent sobs. Mirian stayed there with her, hurting, watching those thin shoulders shake. She thought, *I wonder how long it has been in your life since anyone tried to comfort you. I wonder if anyone ever has.* She thought of something her mother used to say, *"Un poco solo puede ayudar un huevo empollar."* "One can only help a chick to hatch a little." You can open a window for the chick to breathe, but it has to work out of the shell by itself. She moved her chair closer and pulled the sheet up to Magdalena's shoulders. Mirian placed her hand there on the girl's shoulder, prayed silently, and waited. Doña Mirian waited an hour. Magdalena never turned. She lay facing the wall with her back to the world. But after a time, she lay still and perhaps she slept. At the end of an hour, Mirian stood. She replaced the chair, went to the door, paused, and said, "If God permits, I'll return tomorrow."

He permitted. And so she did.

Each morning after settling her household, Mirian would walk out to the road to wait for Alejandro on his way back from Rio Coco toward Jutiapa. He would leave her at the gate of Loma de Luz, where she could wait until visiting hours began. At nine a.m., she would walk through the gate, greeting with poise and grace whichever vigilante was on duty there. For instance, when Tonito was on duty at the gate, she would nod and say, "Good morning, Roberto Antonio," trying not to smile when Tonito would bow too low and say, "Professora Mirian." Mirian had taught elementary school after finishing high school until just before Adolfo was born. Tonito had been one of her first students when she taught the fifth grade. Many still called her Maestra. Tonito insisted on addressing her as "Professora."

When her first cousin's oldest boy, Orlando, was on duty, she might say "Good morning, Lando. Has your mother heard how Felipa did on her exams?"

He would say, "Not yet, Tia Mirian," which is what he had always called her. If old Chan was at the gate, she would say something like, "Good morning, Don Sebastiano, how did you awaken today?" And so on. She would climb the hill and pass through the hospital in the same gracious and dignified fashion, thus to proceed along the corridors until she came to the door of Magdalena's ward. Then with an indefinable but unmistakable shift in bearing, she would walk in as Magdalena's mama *should* walk in. Since Magdalena's mother would never walk in that door, Mirian would do the best she could to stand in her stead.

On most days, Mirian would find Magdalena in bed, sometimes in the chair at her bedside. From the first day, whether in the chair or in the bed, though her face was impassive, she would always be watching for her. Behind those black on black eyes, behind the face that neither smiled nor frowned, nor showed any outward signs, Mirian sensed there was a deep anger and deep despair. But she also knew that Magdalena needed her to come walking in that door. Though Magdalena would grant Mirian neither smile nor greeting... she was always watching the door when Mirian arrived.

But not on this particular day. On this day, the fourteenth day of Magdalena's hospitalization, just after nine a.m., Doña Mirian was turning the corner onto the sala de internados when Dr. Ramon Larios nearly ran right over her. Dr. Larios had been walking *a toda prisa,* "full steam ahead," like a bull with a mission, straight down the hall, eyes fixed on the floor one step ahead, which was unusual for most Hondurans, and quite unusual for Ramon. Compared to North Americans, Hondurans *andan lijano,* they "walk lightly." Ramon, as you might expect from what you've heard so far, generally walks like an upper-class Latino, and that is most assuredly not like a bull with a mission. But Ramon had a lot on his mind just then. The walk and the load on his mind had begun just a few minutes earlier on the ward of Mirian's destination.

Dr. Larios had come onto the ward about twenty minutes earlier. Molly was charge nurse on the ward that morning. Ramon walked to the chart rack and began to gather the charts of the patients he was to make rounds on that morning. He pulled out Magdalena's chart, turned to Molly, and asked, "So, how is our Rainwoman?"

As you might recall, Dr. Larios often flustered Molly. He would say something that would catch her off guard, and she would overreact. She could tell that she was starting down the "caught off guard" trail, but she couldn't quite seem to stop herself from continuing on down it. She responded, "Well, we don't call her the Rainwoman anymore. Her name is Magdalena."

"So I see. But her *apellido?* What is her last name?"

Caught off guard again, Molly answered more sharply than she meant to, "Yes, I know what an apellido is. We just don't know hers … uhm … yet."

Ramon tried to steer the conversation back toward less prickly ground by making a small joke about the name. "Instead of the Rainwoman, perhaps now we should call her *Magdalena de la lluvia.*"

But now, it was Ramon Larios who felt uncomfortable. He had pushed the joke too far. As a Latin, and a sort of aristocrat at that, he understood much more deeply than Molly, the importance, the significance of a name. As an intelligent and sensitive man, he understood that he had crossed the boundary into exalting his own importance as the *dueño*, "the master," who doles out names, over this powerless woman without one. As a Christian, he sensed that he had belittled the dignity of a person created in the image of God and precious to Him. All of this had occurred to Ramon without conscious deliberation and only required a heartbeat or two of time before he coughed a little self-consciously and said, "Pues, bien, pardon me, and in the second place?"

"Well, physically, medically, she's pretty much a miracle. She's been afebrile, vital signs normal, for days ... at least since last Sunday when I was on last. She's tolerating a regular diet. Her white count was normal yesterday. Chest X-ray is clearing up. Dr. Thompson was even saying that he might take her off antibiotics."

"Did she start the peri-natal protocol?"

"Yep, she's on her fourth day for both the AZT and the Nelfinavir. She seems to be tolerating it fine."

"Is there something else?"

"Well, yeah, I guess so. Emotionally, spiritually, she seems as hard and dead as a rock. I can't tell whether she's depressed, or autistic, or has PTSD from the hypothermia, but it seems like she's just mad as hell." Ramon raised one eyebrow at this interesting turn of a phrase, but Molly never even slowed down. "She never talks. She never smiles. She just stares at you with those hard black eyes. The only person she really seems to even notice is Doña Mirian, the mother of the boy who found her. She visits her most every day. But, I don't think Magdalena has said two words even to her."

"Does she know she has AIDS? Or at least, I should say, ARC?"

"Uhm…I can't tell really. Dr. Kevin tried to explain it to her when he started the peri-natal prophylaxis, but he was pretty technical, and I don't know if she got it. He sent Pastor Lazaro in to talk to her, but she just turned her back on him."

"Very well, at any rate, we must do the C-section on Thursday, and I have to try to explain it to her. Would you like to accompany me?"

If the truth were told, Molly did not want to "accompany" Dr. Larios in to watch him tell her that he had to operate to protect the baby from the AIDS virus, but she didn't say so. She figured that it was part of the job and followed him into Magdalena's ward room.

Dr. Larios stood at Magdalena's bedside in his nice clothes and shined shoes and pressed coat. They were separated by about three feet of air, and by an almost uncrossable gulf of education, experiences, and social status. Still, Ramon was a good doctor really, and what he was trying to do was a difficult thing, no matter where you come from. He calmly explained that the tests had shown that she had the HIV virus and that in order to protect the baby from getting the virus at the time of delivery he needed to operate to remove the baby from the womb before he passed through the birth canal. His voice was gentle and kind, but Magdalena stared straight ahead, her eyes boring holes in the air, and said nothing. Ramon continued. "In order to protect the baby (and you) as much as we can, Dr. Thompson began the medicines to fight the virus several days ago. He told you about this, right?" Magdalena still made eye contact only with the space in front of her, and her face didn't register a thing, but she nodded her head once in apparent response to the question. Ramon continued. "The ultrasound shows that the baby is now ready to be born, and so all is ready. We are planning to do the Caesarian operation on Thursday. Do you understand all of this?" Magdalena said nothing but kept staring straight ahead, not looking at Ramon.

After twenty or thirty seconds of silence (which felt much longer), Molly said, "Magdalena, do you understand the doctor?"

Magdalena, still staring ahead, paused another few long seconds, then nodded again. Now Ramon continued, "We must do this for the good of the baby … okay?" Magdalena again nodded after a few long seconds. A few seconds more, and Ramon, anxious to be done with this painful, mostly one-sided interchange, unconsciously took his hands from behind his back and placed them in the pockets of the doctor's armor, his pressed, long, white coat, and said, "Well then, we'll plan to do the operation on Thursday then. Good day, Magdalena." He took a step back from the bedside then turned and headed for the door.

Molly began to follow him out of the room, but as she passed the bed, Magdalena caught her by the arm. "Moli?" A little startled that Magdalena should speak, let alone know and remember her name, Molly stopped in her tracks while Ramon Larios hurried on out of the room. Out here at Loma de Luz, most patients of Magdalena's socio-economic status (which most patients out here are) called Molly *enfermera* or *licenciada*. Or, maybe if they had been in the hospital long enough, they called her *enfermera* Moli. Sometimes she was mistakenly called *doctora*, or, if they knew her name and it was not in a hospital setting, *Doña Moli* (even though she had never been married). But it was a very rare thing for a patient to call her just simply "Moli" particularly someone who had not spoken in two weeks. So Molly was still shaking her head at the oddity of this woman while she found a chair and pulled it up to the bedside. It is also uncharacteristic of a Honduran, particularly one of the rural poor, and particularly a woman, to be blunt and direct. But Magdalena continued in her differentness.

She looked straight into Molly's face this time, her expression still fixed and hard, but her eyes were blurred by tears. She said directly, "That doctor just said that I have *el SIDA,* the AIDS, true?"

"Well, he said that you have the AIDS virus."

"Yes, but that means the same thing once you get sick, right?"

"Well, sort of."

Magdalena's grip weakened and she said, almost in a whisper, "Yes, it seems that I knew that." Then her eyes refocused, and her grip and her voice strengthened as she continued, "But the baby doesn't have it yet? Is that true?"

"Well, probably the baby doesn't have the virus yet. That is why they want to operate to try to keep the virus from the baby. It would be more likely for him to get the virus if he were born through the birth canal." Magdalena nodded and opened her mouth to say something, but a sob came out instead. She choked it back. A tear rolled down one cheek. Unseeing, she stared straight ahead. After a few seconds, she said quietly, "*¿Porque?*" "Why?"

Molly wasn't sure whether Magdalena was asking why she had the AIDS virus, or why the baby didn't, or why God would let her get the AIDS virus, or why she would now be alive when she had been so close to death...only to be facing death again. She wasn't sure what to say or do. She just said silently, "Oh Lord," and stood there wishing she could offer some comfort. It was at this moment when Doña Mirian appeared at the door. She had just nearly collided with Dr. Larios as he came charging down the corridor. She had received his distracted "Pardon!" and come straight on to the room. Molly turned and walked over to where Mirian waited in the doorway. She explained that the doctor had told Magdalena that ... well, that she had a virus, and that in order to protect the baby from the virus, they were going to do the Caesarian operation. They planned to operate on Thursday.

Mirian was no one's fool, and she knew that for Magdalena, "a virus" meant the SIDA, the AIDS virus. Mirian, also a sometimes unusually direct Honduran woman, asked Molly this ... and Molly nodded. Mirian marched right over and sat down next to Magdalena. She took her hand and told her, "*Oh mi amor, mi corazón.* I feel it so much ... I'm so sorry."

Magdalena put her arm around Doña Mirian's waist, put her head in Mirian's lap, and just wept her heart out.

# CHAPTER ELEVEN

Lo, all these things and more worketh God often
times with man to bring his soul from the pit to be
enlightened with the light of the living.

Job 33:29–30

"Why?"

Mirian and Magdalena were alone now in the little sala of four beds. Mirian was seated at the bedside
with her hand on Magdalena's head. Magdalena still
lay with her head in Mirian's lap, with tears now drying on her face. With the wisdom that raising seven
children brings, Mirian knew that it was time to wait
for Magdalena to finish the question.

"Why would you believe in a God who would
let me live, then to have the SIDA, then to die and
leave my baby? Why would you believe in that kind
of God?"

Mirian thought for a moment and answered the

question with a question. "Are you going to have the operation?"

"Yes."

"But it will cost you great pain, and you might die from it. Why would you do that?"

"*Pues* ... so the baby can live."

After a few quiet seconds, Mirian said, "That is the kind of God I believe in." Magdalena lay still a few more seconds and then moved away back onto the bed. She turned her back to Mirian and lay there unmoving with her face to the wall. A few minutes later, Mirian rose and said, "I will see you again in the morning, God willing." Magdalena said nothing, and Mirian walked slowly from the quiet room.

That day was a Tuesday. And, like most Tuesdays, despite all the fear, anger, confusion, and sorrow that it must have held for Magdalena, Tuesday came and went and was followed by Wednesday. Wednesday morning started sort of like a play that had been revised overnight. The characters were mostly the same, but their lives had changed. Ramon Larios made rounds about the same time but just read through Magdalena's chart, seemed preoccupied, and left the ward a few minutes later. He passed Doña Mirian again, and they greeted each other courteously, but this morning they didn't nearly crash into each other in the hospital hallway. They passed each other just as Mirian was entering the front door of the hospital.

Molly was charge nurse on the ward again this morning, but this extra few minutes gained by Ramon leaving early gave Molly a chance to say to Magda-lena what she had been rehearsing when she couldn't sleep the night before. Molly walked into the room and was relieved to see that one of the other women now staying in the little ward with Magdalena was off to the bathroom. The little old diabetic lady admit-ted to get her blood sugar under control was sitting out in the chapel courtyard, visiting with whoever else was passing the time out on the benches there or who happened to be strolling by. The woman recu-perating from a hysterectomy two days earlier was still sleeping, so Molly did not have to share her speech with any audience but Magdalena.

She stood by Magdalena's bedside, took a deep breath, and launched into what she thought she had to say. "Magdalena, good morning." Magdalena looked up at Molly and nodded. Molly continued, "Listen, I've thought about your question from yes-terday, and I still don't know with what respect you were asking the question, 'Why?' And I don't know if I could answer if I did. But, I'm pretty sure that you are really mad at God, and maybe mad at your-self... and maybe I know something about how you feel."

Magdalena just stared at her and thought, *How could you know how I feel? I don't think your worst day was as bad as my best.* Of course she didn't say that, but she sure thought it. With no encouragement com-ing forth from Magdalena, Molly took a deep breath and pushed ahead to say what she had wrestled with the night before. "Maybe you are thinking that I couldn't know how you feel and that nothing bad has ever happened to me. But maybe my childhood was pretty hard too. And maybe when I was sixteen years old, I found out I was pregnant, and I was scared and didn't know what to do and I—" Molly choked a little here, then swallowed and continued. "And I had an abortion. You know what I'm saying? I looked that word up last night." (You must remember that this conversation, like many that I have written here in English, was actually in Spanish, and that this was not Molly's primary language.)

Magdalena nodded. Molly's hurt had caught her attention. Molly went on. "I thought that it would take care of my problem, make it go away, and I would just forget about it. But, I couldn't forget about it. I couldn't forget, and I couldn't forgive myself. I got so sick and mad at myself and mad at God for not stopping me and for judging me. I got so sick that I thought about killing myself."

Magdalena thought about those last days in the stinking old house in Colonia Rivera Hernandez. She thought about the rusty razor on the windowsill. She wondered at how this woman could have ever been that low. Magdalena, who had been shaken by these memories of not so long ago realized that the nurse was still talking. *La Enfermera* Molly had said a word slowly that Magdalena did not know. She was asking Magdalena if she was pronouncing the word right. Magdalena didn't know the word, *alabaster,* and made a little shrug. Molly was saying that someone had told her a story about Jesus and a woman with an alabaster box. Magdalena didn't know what she was talking about, but she listened as Molly went on. She said that this woman was like them, that she was "dying for forgiveness." She said, "That woman's story touched me deep inside. I thought, *If she can be forgiven of so much, then maybe I can be too.* And, anyway, I was tired of being mad at God. And so, I prayed a prayer with my friend and asked if I could be forgiven like that, and then I knew that I was. And then I knew that I could just let go of all of the dirty things that had been done to me ... that I could forgive for them too. And oh, Magdalena, to forgive and to be forgiven, that was so much better than the holding on to the anger. If I had an alabaster box with all that I owned in it, I would have done what she did. I would have broken it and poured it out on my pardoner with joy. That is what started me on the road that led me to become a nurse, the road that led me here."

Another few moments of silence surrounded Molly and Magdalena. This one was not an uneasy silence. Magdalena just didn't know what to say, so she said nothing. Molly broke the silence. "Well, when you're tired of being angry, let me know. Maybe I could help." Magdalena could tell that this was important to Molly: that telling this story had cost her something. But she found it all a little confusing, so she just nodded. Molly touched her hand and said, "I'll be on the ward all day." Magdalena nodded again, and Molly turned and walked back out the door. Again, Molly met Doña Mirian at the same door. Once again they exchanged salutations as Mirian entered and Molly left.

Mirian greeted Magdalena, who nodded. Mirian sat and asked, "Were you talking with the young *enfermera?*"

Magdalena brushed right past the question. Obviously bothered, she said, suddenly, almost shouting, "What do these people want from me! What am I to them?" "Do they think because they're caring for me that I should become like them? Give them what they want for being so *blanco?*"

Finally, I think, Mirian was offended in this. Or, perhaps she thought that the self-serving anger of her newly adopted ward had gone on long enough. She turned to Magdalena and said, "Child, I think that you rate your importance too highly in this. Did you know that that nurse out there stayed up with you for three nights when you were almost dead? Many of these people here have cared for you for weeks now without the least sign of gratitude from you. Have you stopped to think that all of those who will be in the operating room with you tomorrow will be exposing themselves and maybe their families also to the risk of the virus that you carry? I am not a missionary, but it seems to me that they don't care for you to get something from you. Perhaps it is not so much about you after all. Perhaps they take care of you because they care to serve their God, the God who cares for you and for me for reasons only He knows. We both know that you have nothing you can pay for this. But the least that you could do is have the decency to be civil."

Like a schoolteacher reprimanding a wayward pupil, Mirian had been leaning toward Magdalena, stiff backed, feet apart, hands on her knees. Having sufficiently discharged her lecture, she sat back, folded her hands in her lap, crossed her ankles under the chair, and waited. Magdalena made no apology, yet she made no retort.

She sat up in bed quiet and pensive. Presently she asked in a voice now subdued, "Do you know what is alabaster?"

Mirian raised her eyebrow and said, "Yes it is a white stone, like ceramic or porcelain."

"Oh." After a pause Magdalena asked another question. "Do you know the story of the woman with a box of alabaster?"

Doña Mirian frowned pensively over the question for a moment. Then her expression changed to reflect the resolution of the riddle. Smiling a private smile, she said, "Yes. Would you like to hear it?"

Magdalena nodded.

Mirian knew the story well, but the teacher in her wanted to read passages directly from Luke 7. She had a well-worn Bible of her own, but it was at home. So she crossed over to the chaplain's office and returned with a borrowed Bible. Then, sometimes reading, sometimes expanding upon the story, Mirian thoroughly presented a careful exegesis, a tale like a well-worn walking stick; seamless and comfortable, yet solid and meaningful. It was the story of a woman Mirian seemed to know well, like a neighbor or a cousin, a powerless woman, an outcast with no kin and no protector, a woman in a society run by men, men who either used her or despised her or both. But there was one man who neither used her nor despised her nor ignored her. That man, a carpenter's son, was somehow regarded as a prophet and walked in the moral authority to forgive. In the presence of the religious authorities that despised her, this woman, in her desperation, came to this Jesus as if he were her kinsman redeemer, weeping with her alabaster box.

Knowing the Pharisee's hostility but not afraid of the consequences, this carpenter's son told the judge and his friends a parable of two debtors, one forgiven of a small debt, the other of a great debt. Then he asked them which of the two would love the forgiving moneylender more. Then he said, "For this reason I say unto you, her sins, which are many, have been forgiven, for she loved much; but he who is forgiven little loves little."

Mirian continued with the tale, "As we say here, *'El perro que grita es el golpeado.'*" (The dog that yelps is the one that was hit). "It must have stung them because they said to each other, 'Who does he think he is, forgiving sins?' Still not regarding their scorn, he turned to the woman and said, 'Woman, your faith has saved you. Go in peace.'"

Something about the moral power of this man must have caught Magdalena's attention. Something about the way he stood up for the woman and treated her with the dignity of recognition must have opened her heart. Something about the way he offered her forgiveness, the thing that she most needed, must have touched something sleeping inside Magdalena. We don't know just what happened next. As Mirian always said later, "That would be for Magdalena to share." But presently, Mirian walked down the corridor to the nurse's station and called, "Enfermera Molly."

"Yes, Doña Mirian."

"Magdalena has something she would like to share with you."

As Molly walked into the room, she was once again caught off guard by something completely unexpected from Magdalena, something she had never seen her do. She was smiling. She held out her hand to Molly and said, "I want to thank you. Now I understand the alabaster box."

*"Ya le recibí, y ya recibí su perdón."*

"Oh Magdalena," she said, "that makes me so happy for you. Can I sit and say a prayer for you?" And she did…

This completely unassuming string of personal interactions and private conversations and even more private prayer did not look like much on the outside. Yet it was the culmination of all of the choices and consequences, all of the interactions and interventions of Magdalena's life leading up to this quiet choice of the road less traveled. Though her life so far may have been nasty, brutish, and short, imagine that this may have been the necessary down payment for her eternal soul. It may have been a pretty steep initial payment, but eternity is a long time. I'm sure that Jesus of Nazareth said it best. "For what will it profit a man if he gains the whole world and forfeits his soul? Or what will a man give in exchange for his soul?"

There is one last part to consider in this pivotal chapter of Magdalena's life. This too took place with a few people in a quiet place. This too involved sacrifice and risk and brought forth a new life. And, only part of this too, would be proper to tell. On Thursday morning, Doña Mirian had made sure that she would reach the gate, be allowed to pass through the gate, and climb the hill to the hospital before visiting hours. She had convinced Alejandro, the lechero, to begin his rounds a little earlier that morning in order to arrive at the gate at seven a.m.

Old Chan was the *vigilante de turno* at the gate. The day before, Molly had written a note to the vigilantes authorizing Mirian to pass when she arrived early in the morning. When Doña Mirian carefully stepped down from the cab of Alejandro's truck, straightened her dress, and walked up to the gate, she greeted him. *"Buenos Días, Don Sebastiano, cómo almaneció ?"* (How did you awaken?)

*"Con el gozo del Señor, hermanita."* (With the joy of the Lord, little sister.) Sebastiano asked after the health of her family. Mirian said that they were all fine. She presented her pass, which Don Sebastiano frowned at and studied a little uneasily. Old Chan read the printed word very slowly in the best of light,

but his reading glasses were at home, and this note was handwritten in cursive. Doña Mirian explained that she was going up early since Doña Ondina Aleman's granddaughter was to have surgery. Don Chan brightened and said, "Oh yes, to give to light the baby." (The customary way to say "give birth" in this part of the world is to *dar a luz,* literally, "to give to light," or "bring to the light".) Mirian was not the least surprised that he should know this. There was very little that passed as private information in these rural communities and even less that was considered so by Old Chan.

Mirian took her leave and walked steadily up to the hospital in the soft morning light. She found Magdalena still in her bed on the ward, but the operating nurse was starting an IV in preparation for surgery. Mirian watched and waited in the doorway. Magdalena's face was set and unflinching while the needle and canulla were passed through the skin and into the vein; then the canulla was threaded up the vein. She looked hard and unreachable as she had all these days since awakening in the hospital. The needle was removed, the canulla taped in place, and then the operating room nurse straightened up at the bedside. Magdalena's face softened and brightened. She looked up to Mirian in the doorway and smiled like the dawning of the day.

The operating nurse was a missionary of some years of experience. She asked Magdalena if it would be all right if she prayed with her before surgery. She asked every patient that, and as you might imagine,

most every patient before surgery said, "Yes, please."
Though a change was underway in Magdalena, it did
not mean that she would suddenly become open and
loquacious. But she did nod her assent, and did so
still smiling. The nurse asked Magdalena if she was
a *creyente,* a "believer." Magdalena, new to all of this,
did not understand the question because she did not
know the jargon. She just returned a puzzled look
and wondered, *A believer of what?*

The nurse was a sensitive woman, and so noticed
Magdalena's puzzlement. She clarified the question.
"Are you a believer in Jesus, a follower of Jesus?"

Magdalena, of course had known many men
named Jesus. Still, though she was new to this, she
caught on quickly enough.

She brightened and responded, "The Jesus of the
woman that gave the alabaster box? Yes, I know him
since yesterday."

The nurse from the operating room had both
excellent Spanish and an abiding knowledge of the
story. From some years of experience in listening for
His voice, she was prompted to do something she
had not planned. She smiled, leaned across the bed,
and kissed Magdalena on the forehead, and said,
"Like that woman, I think that Jesus cares for you
very much." This was just what Magdalena needed
to hear, just what she needed to know. The nurse
then offered up thanks to Him for caring for Magdalena and a petition from the heart that He would
watch over Magdalena in surgery, and that He might
be honored by what Magdalena did with her life, and

that the baby would be blessed and would be a blessing (or words to the that effect). Magdalena nodded an "amen," and then struggled over onto the gurney to be taken directly down the corridor and into *quiró-fano,* the "operating room." Before she was passed through the door and into the corridor, they paused with the gurney beside Doña Mirian. She also bent, kissed Magdalena on the forehead, and said, "Don't worry, *cariña,* you'll be fine ... and the baby too. I'll wait for you here."

Magdalena, though still smiling, gripped Mirian's hand as if it were her last hope. Then she said softly, almost in a whisper, "Thank you." She relaxed and let go and watched the ceiling pass by as they wheeled her down to the operating room.

Once inside, Magdalena's first sensation was that it was cold. Her second was that it smelled strange and everything seemed alien and sterile. The doctors and nurses and technicians were kind but serious. To add to the strangeness of it all, everyone wore masks and strange hats. Several helped her move sideways onto the table/bed in the middle of the room. Then they wheeled out the bed she had come in on. This left Magdalena feeling very much alone, lying on that hard, cold, narrow little table in the middle of that big strange room. But the woman stationed near her head with the big bank of machines and tubes spoke to her about the mask that was going over her face and about the oxygen and the breathing. Though she wore a mask covering her mouth and nose like all the others, Magdalena recognized her voice as the doctora who had come to her room the afternoon before and told her that she was going to be giving her drugs to make her sleep.

Magdalena tried to pay attention to what the doctora was telling her about the tubes and the gases in the plastic mask she was holding over her face, but she was distracted by people putting things on her and moving her arms and feet. They were strapping her arms down, and Magdalena felt panic begin to rise from her gut to her throat. Then she heard one of the doctors say to the doctora at the head of the table, "Sandi, let's go ahead and pray now before you put her down." This was in English, so of course Magdalena did not understand what he was saying, but she recognized this voice too. This was the surgeon who was going to operate. Though she had not been particularly gracious to him before, it gave Magdalena some degree of comfort to know that he was there. It was then that he began to pray. He prayed in Spanish. Later, she could not recount exactly what were the words that he had prayed, except that he asked God, "To comfort this little sister, to give good results to the operation, and to protect the baby." She agreed fervently inside about this. He then asked God to protect everyone who was in the room. Until that moment, Magdalena had not thought much about the fact that these people were putting themselves at risk for her and for the baby. She had been too scared, and this was a bit too much to take in at one time. But these thoughts distracted her from her own fear until the surgeon said, "And may you be glorified in this new life that is about to be born." Magdalena then felt something burning her arm, and she remembered no more.

In many ways, operating is like dancing... and each operation a particular dance. Each person knows their particular part in the dance. After induction of anesthesia, the primary surgeon leads. Following the dance metaphor, a caesarian section is like a rumba. For most of the operation, the primary surgeon and the first assistant trade off complementary and opposite parts. Dr. Larios was the primary surgeon, and for this operation he had asked Dr. Ragland to assist him. An older missionary surgeon of broad experience, Dr. Ragland had danced past his cocky years, past his demanding years, and well into his most valuable years. He was an overall steadying influence in the operating theater, and Dr. Larios asked him to assist particularly in operations that most needed a smooth, straight-toward-the-goal progression. This was one of those occasions, for, if like a dance, this Caesarian in particular also needed to be like a minuet, each movement synchronized and calculated, nothing ad lib, no confusion to the last note.

Every operation is a calculated risk. But an operation on a patient with an imminently transferable infectious disease, such as viral hepatitis or one with such grave consequences as AIDS, is also a calculated risk for everyone in the room. And, for this operation, as Dr. Larios's prayer had inferred, everyone in the room had agreed to be included in that risk. More than the double gloves, more than the eye protection, and more than the "sharps protocol," everyone's safety, from the patient to the baby to the circulating nurse, everyone's safety depended upon this steady, cooperative progress, no extra motions, no distractions. As Dr. Larios's prayer was answered, this is just how it went. And, as Dr. Larios's prayer was concluded, presently God was indeed glorified. A new creation ... just for a part of a second, His newest, was brought out and held up into the light.

Once again, the youngest son of Adam filled his lungs for the first time with the air of this earth. Once again, the youngest son of Adam returned that air in the first cry of joy and anger, fear and hope, announcing to the world his existence for the glory of God. And, once again, he was then wrapped up and passed off to a woman waiting to hold him, make much over him, and pat him on the butt, a woman whose heart lifted at this sound no matter how many times she had heard it before.

# CHAPTER TWELVE

Who laid the cornerstone, when the morning stars sang together and all the sons of God shouted for joy?

Job 38:6–7

Life in the campiña, "the countryside" of the North Coast of Honduras is hard, most always hard. It isn't always bad, but it is pretty much always hard. *Siempre la lucha,* "always a battle," they say. But sometimes, sometimes there is a truce. Sometimes the light is kind, the air is cool, and the insects are few.

In between the *always wet* of winter and the *forever hot* of summer, in between the mud and the dust, there is a truce; there is respite. However fleeting it might be, there is spring.

Spring usually comes to the North Coast of Honduras early in the month of February. She usually leaves long before her welcome wanes in that same month. In the first week after the last winter

storm, the whole world seems to stand at the door
and drip. The whole world sings with the sound of
running water, water falling downhill, water going
to ground. The sky doesn't seem to know whether to
laugh or weep over this passage. Then the sun breaks
through and colors all golden a world wakened and
dressed in every shade and hue that God made green.
A contrary wind bucks and backs and skips in all
directions like the big-eyed colts born in this season, more propulsion than guidance, more legs than
sense.

Flurries of pale lavender madreado blossoms
blow sideways across the drying dirt roads to collect
like patches of pale lavender snow. *Siempre la lucha,*
"life is a battle." Bur sometimes it is spring. Sometimes it is spring, and there is enough to eat and no
one in the family is sick, and there might even be a
little money in the house. Such a time finally came
for Magdalena ... well, except for maybe the money.

Hospital Loma de Luz was built out in the
campiña proper, out in the campo, out in *el medio de
quien sabe donde,* "the middle of nowhere," if you will.
Though there are close to sixty villages within about
a half day's walk, none of them are much bigger than
one thousand residents (and less than one fifth of
them have electricity; less than one fifth of them
are accessible by automobile). The closest village is
Lucinda, about a mile from the front gate. The next
closest is San Luis, about two and a half miles, then
Balfate, three miles away, and so on. There are few
spare rooms in these villages, and unless you have

friends or family who will take you in, there is basically no place for other poor Hondurans on foot and from outside the area to stay...even if they could afford to do so. So, fairly early in its development, Loma de Luz had built a small Colonia of little guest houses. These were built for housing patients and patients' families, who for various reasons needed to stay near the hospital, but not in the hospital. This little neighborhood of houses was called El Alberge de Sanctuario, or just "Sanctuary."

There came a day in spring, about a week after the Caesarian operation, when they brought Magdalena to a little house in Sanctuary. She no longer required hospitalization, but she still needed medical care. Besides, she had nowhere else to go.

Actually Doña Mirian had offered, had almost insisted, that she come stay with her family. But, for whatever her reasons, Magdalena had steadfastly refused. Perhaps it was pride. Perhaps it was fear of being too far from the hospital with the baby. Whatever the reasons were, we'll never know. Though Magdalena was changing, was changed, she was still not what one might consider a great communicator. She just said, "No, no thank you. I think the baby and I should stay close."

So there came a day in spring, about a week after the Caesarian operation, that they brought Magdalena to a little house in Sanctuary. They gave her sheets and towels, and they gave her some food. The nurse would check on her each day, usually a nurse she knew; sometimes it was Molly. Mirian visited every other day, and there was medicine to take and the baby to care for. She tried not to think of what might happen later. For now, just for today and maybe tomorrow, there was respite from la lucha. For now, just for today and maybe tomorrow, she had "arrived at her dreams" as they say. She had come to that safe place, clean and light, a place with enough food, a place where it didn't seem as though something terrible was always just about to happen.

Here in this little house on the edge of a pasture, the morning sun cast its net in through the window on the southeast wall, and the evening sun drew it back again through the window in the northwest wall. The water was clean. The adobe walls were thick and cool. The roof gave good shelter from the midday sun and from the last squalls off the sea.

Magdalena had a lot to sort out. Perhaps she needed time alone to do just that. She had come as close to death as one can go this side of the veil and still return. In a very real sense, Magdalena had been reborn. And it wasn't just in her body that she had nearly died and been reborn. As the prophet Isaiah had proclaimed so long ago, her spirit which had for so long "walked in darkness," had now "seen a great light."

A sudden light can be disorienting. In the same way that our eyes must adjust to a sudden light, our heart must adjust to an unexpected second chance. With that sudden light, that unexpected second chance, Magdalena had a new relationship to sort out. She knew amazingly little of this man, this "Jesus of the woman with the alabaster box." From Doña Mirian and from the chaplain and the nurses who came out to visit her in the little house in Sanctuary, she learned a little more. It was from Mirian that she gained the revelation that this Jesus was God's own son: that His *evangelio* and His followers would live forever. This gave Magdalena a lot to think about, a lot more to sort out that she had never considered before. When it finally dawned on Magdalena that this applied to her, it gave her back something that she had lost long ago. It gave her hope.

Then there was the baby. What does a young mother feel about her baby? Well, I suppose I could guess, but whenever possible, I've tried not to guess in the telling of this story. I've tried to do the work necessary to get as close as I could to the bottom of things. So, I've asked those who should know. In this case, I have asked mothers about their feelings for their babies. Across the board, they seemed to be surprised by the joy.

"I never knew that I could love someone so much."

"I couldn't believe he was so beautiful."

"I never thought someone would need me so much."

"I had this overwhelming desire to protect and nurture her."

"She makes me so happy I feel my heart will break."

"I'm just in awe."

Magdalena felt all of these fierce and gentle, deep

and lovely feelings. And I suppose that she might have been surprised by the joy of this love even more than most. You might remember that Magdalena had had little experience with love of any kind in her brief and brutal life. She knew nothing of a love of this depth and purity. It sometimes scared her, sometimes took her breath away. It surely surprised her.

So this was the way that Magdalena spent the first few weeks of a new spring in a new little house. She spent those green and golden days trying to *acostumbrarse,* "to realign," to familiarize herself with a new chance at life, a new faith, a new outlook, a new timeline that went on forever. It was finally true that she "lay down with hope and awakened with joy." But most often it was also true that she lay down exhausted and awakened tired. For, lest we forget, she had a baby to care for. And babies, while they may be small packages of joy, make a great mountain of work. Why, they can't wipe their own nose ... or anything else. Magdalena was all there was to care for this hungry, helpless, messy little package. So they spent these weeks together healing and growing, eating and sleeping, making a mess and cleaning up, joy and drudgery, starlight and daylight. They were so close that there was no clear line of distinction where the mother ended and the baby began.

Yet there had to come a day when the bond would be broken. As Robert Frost put it so beautifully, "So dawn goes down to day, Nothing gold can stay."

It began on a morning in April. Magdalena felt a little muddled, a little achy, a little pain in the head, a little fever. She thought that perhaps it was the *gripe,* (a cold or the flu). She thought that this would pass; if the baby would just sleep all the way through the night. When Mirian came to visit in the middle of the morning, Magdalena told her that she felt tired and thought that maybe she had the gripe. She asked Mirian if she could watch the baby while she slept a little.

Once, some years ago, I was carrying a two-year-old boy up a stream. His mother, who was carrying another of her children, was momentarily around the bend and out of sight. Not too happy with this development, yet still trying to keep a brave face on it, the little boy suggested, "Don't you think we should wait for the mommy? Not "Mommy" or "my mommy," but, "the mommy," as in "the only mommy in all of God's creation." In just this way, Magdalena had no other name for the baby yet. She thought of her child as *el bebé* not as in "the very young child," but as in "the only baby in all of God's creation."

So Mirian watched Magdalena sleep while *el bebé, el varoncito, el primogénito,* "the baby," did everything but sleep. "The baby" was nearly six weeks old now, and his features were becoming distinctive. He had his mother's frank and open eyes. He had her crooked smile, her stubborn set of the jaw, and a dimple all of his own. The nose was apparently someone else's … and the hair was just too early to say, except that there was a lot of it, and it kind of went in all directions at once. Mirian's mother's heart warmed as he lay there in her lap and broke out that crooked smile. With their eyes locked on, she said to *el bebé,* "It's time that you had a name of your own. I'll have to help your mami discover it." Mirian stayed a couple of hours while Magdalena slept. Presently, the baby slept too. Doña Mirian had other children that she needed to return to, so she placed the sleeping baby in the *cuna* (crib) beside his mother in the corner of the little house and quietly closed the front door behind her.

Later in the afternoon of the same day, the nurse came to check on Magdalena and the baby. On a rotating schedule, a nurse came to Sanctuary each day to check on the various patients, depending upon who was staying there at the time. The nurse came to change dressings, to see that medicines were being taken properly, to note problems or progress. But, more than anything else, the nurse came to listen and to share a little of her time. The nurse that day happened to be Molly. When Molly came to *casita* number six, she stepped up onto the little front porch and tapped on the door, calling, "Magdalena, *buenas tardes.*" She waited a minute or two, and, hearing nothing, she knocked a little harder and called out a little louder, *"Magdalena, está despierta?"* After a few minutes more with no response, she tried the front door and found it unlocked. Opening it, she looked in and said, "Magdalena?" Across the little room, she saw her lying asleep in the bed with her back to the door. The baby was lying in the bed beside her between his mamma and the wall. Molly thought about waking her but only for half an instant. They both looked so tranquil and close. She decided they needed the rest and did not disturb them, so she quietly closed the door and went her way.

The next morning, when Doña Mirian returned, she knew right away that something was not right. The baby was crying for all he was worth, and by now had worked himself up into quite a mad tear. Yet Magdalena just lay there on her side, bent around him with her neck held stiffly in an unnatural position. She had her hand on the baby's chest, but just lay there very still. She did not move when Mirian called her name nor even when she touched her shoulder. But when Mirian reached over to lift the crying baby, Magdalena turned and reached out with her right arm, groping blindly with her eyes tightly shut. Mirian tried to calm her. "It's all right. It's me. I have the baby."

Magdalena lay still and softly groaned with her right arm over her eyes. Her speech was slow and slurred. She sounded sleepy or drugged as she mumbled, "The light! It hurts. My head hurts so much. I can't bear it."

For once, Mirian was unsure of what she should do. The baby needed changing and was hungry. But it was apparent that Magdalena needed medical attention urgently. Should she leave the baby and go get help, or should she take the baby with her? Falling back on the reflex patterns of a lifetime of lesser emergencies, Mirian just did the next right thing, the next thing that needed doing. She cleaned and changed the baby. Then she placed a cool rag over

Magdalena's eyes and the baby at her breast. As she opened the screen door, she spoke over her shoulder. "I'm coming back soon." She turned to ease the door closed behind her and looked back through the screen and across the room. Magdalena hadn't moved, but at least the baby was still and quiet.

Her feet brought Mirian directly to the road of their own accord. Her mind was occupied with what could be the problem with Magdalena and what she could do about it. The road from the Alberge de Sanctuario to the hospital was about a quarter of a mile to travel. It was flat and straight. This was early April. And by that time of year, the dirt road was already getting hard and dusty. By that time of the morning, the cooler land breeze falling down off the mountains had ended, and the sea breeze had not yet turned the tables. Without a breath of breeze, the road lay shimmering under the full weight of the tropical sun.

It was ten o'clock *en punto,* "on the dot," when Mirian arrived at the gate. So, of course, the ten o'clock bus had not yet arrived. The outpatient clinic was in full swing. The nurses were processing the last of the early patients and getting ready for the next wave that would arrive with the bus. Most commonly, patients would address the *tecnica* or the *enfermera auxiliar* first. Mirian, however, walked straight over to the head nurse. The head nurse at triage that morning was Doña Norma. Mirian knew her a little and knew that she could get help most directly through Norma. Mirian quickly said good morning and asked forgiveness for being so direct but explained that she had just come from visiting Magdalena in the casita in the Alberge de Sanctuario, and she was concerned she was gravely ill. Mirian explained how she had found her and what she had observed. Norma said, "I understand. You did the right thing. We'll get help down there as quickly as we can." She then directly called on her radio to the doctor *de Turno*.

The doctor on call was once again, Dr. Kevin Thompson. Dr. Kevin seemed to think for just a minute and then responded, "We should check on her as soon as possible. It sounds like it may be meningitis." With his finger still on the transmit key, it sounded as if he may have been thinking out loud as he added, "Cryptococcal Meningitis." Norma offered on the radio to go get her own car and get down to Sanctuary to check on Magdalena as quickly as she could turn over the ten o' clock arrivals to *Miguel Angel,* the auxiliar. Norma turned to explain this plan to Mirian, but Mirian was already gone, one hundred meters back down the road toward Sanctuary.

Mirian walked right into casita number six without bothering with the knocking or the waiting or the greeting. The baby was crying again. Magdalena lay without moving, eyes half open. Her breathing was shallow and rapid. She seemed to breathe from her belly. As Mirian came into focus beside the bed, Magdalena shifted her eyes toward her. Her head fell weakly in Mirian's direction. She tried to speak but seemed to have trouble forming the words. The right side of her face didn't move. Magdalena raised her right arm, palm upward toward Mirian. The baby boy wrestled and cried on her left side. But her left arm did not seem to be able to move to hold him.

Mirian pulled up the chair to the bedside and leaned in close. Magdalena seemed to make a great effort to gather her thoughts, to make herself understood. She put her right hand on the fretting baby's chest. Still looking at Mirian, she whispered, "*Tómale.*" "Take him." Then with another great effort she got out, "*Cúidale.*" "Care for him."

Not sure that she understood, Mirian reached across the bed, picked up the baby, and sat back in the chair, settling the baby. Magdalena reached out with her right hand and put it on the baby's face and chest. A tear from each eye silently sought gravity, gathered itself, and waited for the fall.

Again Magdalena struggled to collect herself. She struggled for each breath. She struggled for the words. "His name is *Tomás*...who questions." The words came out slurred, and Mirian would not have been able to guess at what Magdalena had said, but she remembered reading to Magdalena about the apostle Thomas a few days before. Magdalena had smiled and said, "I like that one, Tomás, the one who questions." Mirian's face now must have been a puzzle of mixed emotions because with an effort, Magdalena now said a bit more clearly, "Tomás...who questions."

The three of them stayed, just so, for a long few moments, Mirian seated at the bedside holding the quieting baby. Magdalena lay unmoving on the bed with her hand on the baby, her head turned toward them, eyes half open, struggling to breathe. Then Magdalena focused her eyes again on Mirian. She smiled a crooked smile and said rather clearly, *Ya me voy a … casa … mi hogar,* "Going home … I'm going home." Presently, her hand slipped from the baby and into Mirian's lap. She sighed and was still. *La lucha,* the struggle, Magdalena's struggle, was finished.

That is what Mirian told me. That is how I got my name. That is how my mother died.

And always, when Mirian has told me this story, she finished it like this: "Much of your mother's life was difficult, hard, and full of misery. One can surely die of misery. Or your life might turn on a raindrop. Magdalena very nearly died of misery. But she didn't. I believe her life turned on a raindrop. So it didn't end that way. No, it doesn't end … not ever."

# EPILOGUE

Therefore I have declared that which I did not understand, Things too wonderful for me, which I did not know.

Job 42:3

Yes, my name is *Tomás Adolfo Garcia Aleman.* My mother, Magdalena Aleman gave me my first name and my *apellido segundo,* my "second last name." Perhaps Magdalena had not had much opportunity to learn of the lives of the apostles. But she knew of the one who doubted, the one who questioned. From what I have heard, I imagine she named me Tomas in hope or expectation that I might do likewise.

Doña Mirian Ortiz Garcia I have always called "mami." I was in my thirteenth year, the same age that Arturo was when he found my mother, before I learned that Mirian was not my mother by blood. Mirian gave me my second name after the son she had lost. I grew up in the household of Doña Mirian and my papi, Don Nando Garcia. Don Nando gave me my *apellido primero,* my "first last name," when he went through the expensive process to adopt me legally as his son. Though I eventually learned that they were not my parents "of blood," I can honestly say that they never treated me as anything less than their proper son. I owe to them the better part of whoever I have become.

It was from Mirian and Nando that I learned the lessons that a child needs to know, most importantly that there is someone who loves you, no matter what. It was from Mirian that I learned much of the details of this book, my mother's story. Interviewing her for this book, she told me that I owed my mother for more than my life and my first name. It was from Magdalena for certain, she said, that I got my hard head and my crooked smile.

From my papi, Don Nando, I learned what it was to work and what it meant to be a man of your word. It was from Don Nando that I learned that anything of value will cost you something, and that we should give our best to God … not our leftovers. He called this "giving the first cut," or the first fruit of the harvest, *la primicia de la siega.* Don Nando died suddenly while I was in my third year of surgery training in the USA. He was buried before I received the news. I miss that old man terribly.

One last group of people have greatly shaped this story and greatly shaped my life. They are many of the people that I wrote of in this story: the missionaries at Hospital Loma de Luz. As a young child,

Mirian took me to a progressive English as a Second Language course taught by a missionary. I guess I was a pretty good student because they let me enter the bilingual school started by and run by that same missionary. It was there that I found a love for learning and a love for books (including Mr. Frost's poetry). As a boy, I worked for missionaries. When high school aged, I worked afternoons, cleaning up at the hospital. It was a missionary that noticed me there and like the teachers at the bilingual school, he encouraged me to go to university. He and his wife sacrificed to help me pay for costs during the seven long years of medical school in this, my native land.

It was a missionary who helped me with the connections necessary to matriculate to surgical training in the United States. That was old Dr. Sturtz. A few years ago, Dr. Sturtz was retiring. He was planning to return to the USA, but he really didn't know where to go. The home community he had left thirty years before was no longer home. During the thirty years he spent on the mission field in Honduras, he had gradually given up family, friends, and any chance at a fortune in this life.

I asked him then what I had always wondered about missionaries. I asked him, "Why? Why did you come here, and why did you stay spending your working life out here in the campo of someone else's country?"

"Well," he said, "I started out a lot like you, Tomas. I was one of those foolish enough to ask questions. When I was satisfied enough with the why, I would ask the how and the what. When I was a young man, I asked God, "All right then, how can I serve you and make a difference? What do you want me to do? He answered me with this calling, this life. So I guess I'm just one of God's own fools that He sends out to school for asking too many questions, out to where I was needed the most, and where I most needed to be."

That conversation with Dr. Sturtz struck a cord in me. I realized that I had never asked those particular questions. So I put down the question why, and I asked God, "All right then, what do you want *me* to do? How can *I* serve you? How can *I* make a difference?" He answered me with this calling, this life. Now I guess *I'm* just one of God's own fools that He sent back, back to where I was needed the most, to where I most needed to be. Though there aren't many yet, I believe there will be others to follow, others to be sent back to where they are needed the most.

Mirian is seventy-six years old now. Soon after I came back, soon after the last rainy season, she began to fill in the gaps for me of what I knew of my mother's story. One day in February, she told me that thirty years had now passed since the day they found Magdalena out in the rain. When we finished talking, Mirian sat without stirring for a long while. She was looking off to her left and down at the floor, her ankles crossed and her hands lying still in her lap. She has taken to doing that more these last few years, particularly when she is missing Papi.

She finally seemed to realize that I was sitting there with her, and without explaining what she had been thinking of, or where she had wandered, she began in midthought. "Yes," she said, "He gives and He takes away. But He never takes away without giving back a little better. He rescued your mama, and then He took her back again. But He gave us you. Now you've come back to continue what He started with her. You are like the first fruit, Tomas, *la primisia de la siega que sigue la lluvia,* "the first fruit of the harvest that follows the rain."